# DON'T

Penny Kline has worked as a teacher, psychologist and student counsellor. She now writes full time, and has written four books for adults – DYING TO HELP, FEELING BAD, A CRUSHING BLOW and TURNING NASTY. DON'T BREATHE A WORD is her fourth Karen Cady mystery. A WATERY GRAVE, DEATHLY SILENCE and A CHOICE OF EVILS are also published by Hodder Children's Books.

Penny Kline is married with two grown-up children, and lives in Bath with her husband and her dog.

*Also by Penny Kline*

**A WATERY GRAVE
DEATHLY SILENCE
A CHOICE OF EVILS**

# Don't Breathe A Word

## Penny Kline

*Hodder*
*Children's*
*Books*

a division of Hodder Headline plc

A Catalogue record for this book is available from
the British Library

ISBN 0 340 66097 X

Typeset by Avon Dataset Ltd, Bidford-on-Avon, Warks

Printed and bound in Great Britain by
Cox & Wyman, Reading, Berks.

Hodder Children's Books
A division of Hodder Headline plc
338 Euston Road
London NW1 3BH

# *One*

'Have I come at a bad time?' Karen saw Tessie's pale, shocked face and took an involuntary step backwards.

'No, don't go.' Tessie caught her by the arm and pulled her inside the house. 'It's Esme, Mum's friend from the art class.' Her voice trembled a little. 'Someone broke into her bungalow and attacked her. She's dead.'

Mrs Livingstone was standing by the kitchen window and, even at a moment like this, Karen was struck by how alike Tessie and her mother looked. Fair hair, cut in the same style; round, slightly surprised-looking eyes; pastel-coloured clothes. It was almost as if Tessie had modelled herself on her mother, whereas Karen had gone

5

to considerable lengths to look as different as possible from hers.

'Karen, you've heard the dreadful news?' Mrs Livingstone had a crumpled tissue in her hand. 'I had a phone call half an hour ago, from another member of the class. Apparently a neighbour called round at the bungalow. She could see Esme through the frosted glass in the front door, thought she must have had a fall, then found a window open at the back and furniture overturned.'

'How old was she?' It was a pointless question but the only thing Karen could think of to say.

'Sixty-eight. No, sixty-nine, she had a birthday last month. I just can't take it in. Who on earth could have done such a thing?'

Karen had never met Esme Fitch, but she remembered seeing one of her paintings at the annual Art Society exhibition. Tessie had dragged her along and they had trailed round, looking at endless pictures of trees and streams and vases of flowers. Esme Fitch's had been different; a huge, garish picture of a naked woman with a head that was far too small for her body. At the time, they couldn't stop laughing.

'She was always so careful to lock all her doors and windows,' said Mrs Livingstone, 'but I suppose if someone's determined to break in there's nothing anyone can do.'

'Could she have let the person in?' asked Karen. 'I mean, it might have been one of those con tricks when someone says they've been sent round to check the gas. Was anything stolen?'

'I've no idea. You think it was a burglary that went wrong? Yes, what else could it be?'

'Did she have anything valuable in the house? Was anyone seen in the area?' Karen broke off, aware that she was starting to sound more like the police than a sympathetic friend.

'I don't know any details, Karen.' Mrs Livingstone emptied the remains of her mug of tea into the sink. 'Esme was such a dear, so full of life, so involved with all kinds of good causes. And I've never known anyone who had so many friends.'

Karen opened her mouth to ask if she could also have had enemies, but Tessie gave her a look that said: Don't ask any more questions, I'll tell

7

you what you want to know later.

Mrs Livingstone was explaining how the bungalow was in one of the cul-de-sacs that led off from Riverdale Road. 'It backed on to some playing fields. Isn't that exactly the kind of place burglars like? She'd have put up a fight, I know she would, not that she'd have stood a chance.' She moved wearily towards the door. 'I'll be back in a moment, only I promised Margaret I'd phone two other members of the class. It would be awful if they tuned into local radio and heard the news.'

After she left Karen asked if Tessie had known Esme Fitch quite well.

'Yes, I suppose so. Mum really liked her. She was one of those people with terribly strong opinions about everything. If someone disagreed with her she used to go all red in the face and start waving her arms about.'

'I thought your mother said she was a *dear*.'

'Oh, she was.' Tessie struggled to find the right words. 'I mean, she was really kind, always giving people presents, mostly things she'd made or cooked.'

'She was a widow, was she?'

'Oh no, she'd never been married. She didn't seem to think much of men. She used to go on about how women were the tough ones. When she was younger she lived at Stockwood House, but after her parents died it was sold, to pay the death duties, and she had to move into the bungalow off Riverdale Road.'

'Stockwood? Isn't that the place Peter Quayle bought?'

Tessie nodded. 'He's got a flat in Chelsea too, and a villa in Portugal.'

'And he's only thirty-something, and he's made a fortune selling health foods to idiots like Alex.'

Tessie smiled. Mention of Alex had reminded her how Karen's mother and stepfather were on holiday in France. 'What's it like staying with your dad? D'you have to sleep on the floor of the office?'

'No, of course not. There's an old sofa in the sitting-room. Actually, I'm trying to convince him that it could be a permanent arrangement.'

'A live-in member of Cady's Detective Agency? Some hope, Karen, you've tried that one before.'

Karen had stopped listening. 'If Esme Fitch

once lived at Stockwood House she must have been quite well off.'

'Oh, no, I don't think so. She didn't even have a video recorder. I remember her saying television should be banned because it turned people into mindless morons. It seems awful to say it now, but sometimes I thought she was a bit odd.'

'Lots of people don't like television. What did she look like? What kind of clothes did she wear?'

'Trousers,' said Tessie. 'Awful old things, and a shirt that hung down almost to her knees. Under it she'd have a tee shirt, or a jumper if it was cold. They were almost like men's clothes, except she always wore beads round her neck and a brooch with a large blue stone.'

'Fat or thin?'

'Not thin, but definitely not fat. Not very tall. Short grey hair. Look, why d'you want to know all this, what's the point? I'd better go and see if Mum's OK.' She paused, looking slightly shamefaced. 'I was going to collect signatures for the petition, now it doesn't seem right.'

'I don't see why not. Baby seals are far more

appealing than an old woman who's been bashed over the head in her own home.'

'It's nothing to do with seals,' said Tessie coldly, making Karen regret the way she had reacted to hearing about the petition yet again. 'And you don't have to say anything, I know you're all in favour of using animals for experiments in laboratories.'

'I just think, if your child had a fatal illness you'd want a cure found, even if it meant trying out drugs on animals.'

Tessie sighed. 'But there's other ways of testing drugs and most research with animals is completely unnecessary.'

They stared at one another. A woman had been killed and all they could do was have the same argument they'd been having for the past three weeks, ever since Tessie had become obsessed with animal rights. Still, one way or another they had been quarrelling, then making it up, for years, ever since they had first met at primary school, and somehow the fact that they were so different, and disagreed about so many things, had only served to keep the friendship alive.

'Anyway,' said Karen, 'I'm really sorry about Miss Fitch.'

'Yes, I know.' Tessie accompanied her to the front door, then lowered her voice. 'Listen, d'you really think it was a burglar who did it? Only I saw Esme the week before last and she said something rather strange.'

'How d'you mean, strange?'

'She didn't like the police very much. I suppose it was because they once had to lift her off the road when she was demonstrating against live animals being exported. But at other times she'd defend them.' Tessie put on the gruff voice Karen had heard her use before, when she quoted something Esme Fitch had said. 'And I'd like to know what you'd do if someone broke into your house and there was no-one to turn to, no-one to answer your 999 call.'

'You said she said something strange.'

'Yes, I'm coming to that. She'd brought round some homemade lemonade only everyone was out except me. I made her a cup of tea and she was rather quiet, not like she usually was. Then she suddenly asked if I thought the police took any notice of things ordinary members of the public told them or just—'

Mrs Livingstone had finished her phone calls and was coming out into the hallway. Whatever it was Tessie had been going to say would have to wait until later.

When she returned to the flat her father was standing in front of the only mirror in the place, trimming his moustache.

'Someone's been murdered,' she said.

'Presumably you're talking about Riverdale Road.'

'Esme Fitch. Tessie knew her quite well. Her mother went to the same art class.'

'So it was Tessie who told you about it?'

Karen nodded. 'I suppose she must have heard a noise, gone to see who it was and—'

'It may turn out she died from a heart attack.'

'It would still be murder.'

Her father took his jacket off the back of a chair. 'More likely to be manslaughter. A burglar who was apprehended, then had to struggle to break free. The prosecution would have a job proving intention to kill. By the way, if you're going to the shops we need more cheese, only don't get anything fancy, cheddar will do.'

'It's bad for you, eating so much cheese.'

'Oh, rubbish. You and Tessie going out somewhere this afternoon, are you? Don't sit around in here, unless you've some schoolwork to finish.'

'Tessie's collecting signatures in the High Street.'

'What for? No, don't tell me, it'll be something somebody wants to ban. Over there on the table. Card from your mother.'

'What does it say?'

'I'm not in the habit of reading other people's mail.' Then he laughed. 'They broke their journey at somewhere called Angoulême and Alex ate something that disagreed with him.'

The local shopping centre had one remaining supermarket and there were rumours that after the new out-of-town hypermarket opened, it would eventually close and people who were too old or too poor to own a car would have to buy food at expensive corner shops.

Karen consulted her list. Shopping was so boring and they needed far more than just cheese. Bread, biscuits, tea bags, washing-up liquid. As she searched through the bunches of bananas, looking for ones that were neither too green nor covered in disgusting black spots, her thoughts were still absorbed with what had happened to Esme Fitch.

What had she meant when she asked Tessie if the police took notice of what ordinary people told them? Had she found out something important, or had she just been a busybody, eager to report a neighbour for using his home as an office, or failing to renew the road tax on his car?

Further down the supermarket aisle she could see a boy from her school. His name was Josh Bowen, which was all she knew about him apart from the fact that he was a year ahead of her and had won the chess competition. She already knew one guy in that class, Mark Hill, and she couldn't stand him. Josh had a wire basket in his hand but as far as she could see it was empty, and for some inexplicable reason he was stuffing his pockets with packets of kitchen sponges.

As she made her way round the supermarket she managed to keep him in sight, making sure he was sufficiently far ahead not to see her. He was wearing a green army-style jacket and by the time he reached the checkout his pockets were bulging with stuff. Karen thought about Mrs Ingram's course in Ethics and the 'moral dilemmas' she was always on about. If a friend broke the law should your first concern be loyalty to your friend or did you have a duty . . . ? Josh Bowen wasn't a friend, but in any case she had no intention of reporting him.

A fat woman in a purple anorak was making a fuss about her bill. The cupcakes were on special offer but she had been charged the normal rate. Then she produced a handful of '20p off' coupons. Karen kept her eyes fixed on Josh. The store detective couldn't be much good – Josh had made so little effort to disguise what he was doing – but perhaps, with profits down, the supermarket had dispensed with its security staff.

Josh was two places ahead of her in the queue

and she could see his wire basket now contained a packet of digestive biscuits and a tin of chicken soup. His shoulders were slightly hunched so that his collar covered the ends of his straggly brown hair, and when he turned to drop the basket in a rack Karen noticed how the darkness of his eyes was accentuated by the pallor of his skin. The checkout lady handed him his bill and he gave her a ten pound note, put the change in his pocket with all the stuff he had nicked, then left the shop and strolled across the road.

Her first instinct was to abandon her own basket and follow him, but that would mean doing the shopping all over again. Shuffling her feet impatiently, she waited for the old man in front to pay for his pork-pie and packet of tea, then stared at her watch, willing the checkout woman to get a move on. She had her money ready and less than two minutes later she was cramming her shopping into a plastic bag as she rushed through the swing-door, out into the street.

Josh had disappeared. He could have turned a corner or gone into another shop. Karen had no idea where he lived so there was no way she could guess what route he had taken and, in any case, he was unlikely to go straight home with his pockets full of stolen goods. She had seen kids shop-lifting plenty of times, but mostly they took a single item, a bar of chocolate or packet of sweets, then left the shop as quickly as possible. There was something different about Josh. The way he had gone about it, it was almost as if he was inviting a shop assistant to arrest him.

If her father had taken her advice and thrown his old shoes in the dustbin instead of deciding to have them reheeled, she might never have seen Josh again, not until the summer term began. The shoe-repair place was next to a newsagent's and as she was passing she suddenly spotted the green army jacket. He was standing by the paperback books, flicking through the pages of one, but looking in the opposite direction. Then, as Karen watched, he shoved one under his jacket and walked past the man on the till, out into the street. Slowly, methodically, he began emptying his pockets into a litter bin. First the stuff from the supermarket, then the book and something that could have been a magazine. He had his back to Karen and she was sure he was quite unaware she had been watching him. When he walked away she caught a glimpse of his expression. There was something triumphant about it, and also something very angry.

Five minutes later, when she returned to the litter bin, she found the magazine was actually a local street map. It had been roughly folded to show a particular area of the city and one end of a long road had been marked with a cross. If it had not been mentioned earlier in the day she would probably have thought nothing of it. As it was, the letters seemed to jump out and she found herself repeating the name out loud: 'Riverdale. Riverdale Road.'

## Two

Mark Hill was leaning against the wall, eating something wrapped in greasy paper. His slave, Lee Mackenzie, stood a few metres away from him, chewing his nails. As Karen drew closer she could tell from the expression on Mark's face that he was going to jump to the same conclusion he always jumped to if any girl gave him a second glance.

'Hi, how you doing?' He smiled, pushing back the floppy hair that he thought was so irresistible.

'Josh Bowen,' said Karen. 'He's in your class, isn't he?'

'Why d'you want to know? I wouldn't have thought he was your type.'

Lee had joined them. He grinned at Mark, but Mark ignored him.

'He hasn't been at the school all that long, has he?' she continued. 'Didn't he win the chess competition? Only a friend of mine—'

'A friend of yours? That's what they all say.' Mark handed the remains of his burger to Lee, who inspected it, then tossed it in the gutter. 'Moved here about six months ago. Never says a word unless he's forced to. Father's a cop.'

'Really?'

'Yes, really.' Mark fixed his eyes on her in what he thought was a penetrating stare. 'What is all this? Been helping out at the Cady Detective Agency? Oh, no, of course, your friend.' He laughed, wiping his fingers on Lee's sleeve. 'Josh Bowen. Bit of a sad case, I'd say. Got a brother at boarding school.'

'Who told you that?'

'Reckon that's where he'd like to be. S'pose he failed the entrance exam or something.'

'You don't happen to know where he lives?'

Mark glanced at Lee and raised his eyes to heaven. 'You have got it bad. Haven't a clue, but if you track him down I don't reckon you'd have any problem fixing something up. Reckon he'd jump at it.'

Tessie was standing behind the trestle-table, arranging leaflets and making sure the clipboards had pens attached to them. A short distance away from her a large woman, dressed in bottle-green dungarees, was pinning gruesome photographs to a board leaning against a tree. Monkeys behind bars, with gaping mouths that gave the impression they were screaming in agony. Sheep squeezed into lorries. A red-eyed dog sitting forlornly in the corner of a cage.

'Come to help?' Tessie said, using her special animal liberation voice.

'Don't look as if you need any help.' Karen nodded at the team of volunteers.

'Well, at least you can sign the petition. It's nothing to do with medical research, just testing cosmetics and that kind of thing.' Tessie had a new sweatshirt, a pink one with white lettering: 'Animals don't smoke, drink, take drugs, drive cars . . .' The rest of the message was obscured by the trestle-table.

While Karen was reading through the heading at the top of the petition someone she had never seen before came up to Tessie and gave her a hug. Then the two of them started talking about Esme Fitch.

'If I could get hold of the bastard . . .' The man was very tall, dressed in baggy black trousers, black trainers, and an old navy-blue sweatshirt with a hood. The sweatshirt had two badges attached to it. One said 'Say No to Live Exports' and the other had a picture of an otter and the inscription: 'Wildlife Matters'. He and Tessie seemed to know each other pretty well.

'Have the police got any leads?' His voice was soft, almost a whisper.

Tessie shook her head, then turned to Karen. 'Karen, this is Billy. Karen's in my year at school.'

'You knew Esme too?' asked Billy. 'You must be as cut up as the rest of us. She was so active, did so much to help, I could hardly believe it when the newspaper said she was nearly seventy.'

Tessie was gazing admiringly at Billy and now

that Karen had a chance to study him properly she could see why. His hair was an unusual reddish-brown – not as bright as her own but, in her opinion far more attractive – and his skin had the look of someone who spends most of their time out-of-doors, only not doing anything as ordinary as working on a farm, more like an international tennis player or someone who had recently sailed round the world single-handed.

Karen had expected him to join Tessie behind the trestle-table, but she could hear him explaining how he had to speak to someone but hoped to be back in half an hour. As he walked away he was joined by two others: a girl with a minuscule skirt, deliberately torn tights, and beads plaited into her hair, and a man with a round, fat face and small, piggy eyes. They saw Tessie and waved wildly, making Karen feel excluded from a group of like-minded do-gooders.

'Selina and Craig,' said Tessie. 'Craig's a bit of an idiot but he turns up for all the demos. I think they all met up when Billy had a brief craze for bungee jumping. Craig and Selina used to go along, just to watch.'

'Oh, I met someone who did that.' Karen watched the three of them join the throng of shoppers waiting to cross the road. 'Ted something or other, I forget his other name. Alex bought a car from him. Anyway, you've kept Billy rather quiet. What's his other name?'

'Henderson. Why? What d'you mean?' Tessie tried to look mystified. 'Actually, his real interest is conservation. He studied Ecology at university but the course wasn't much use so he left and joined a community in Wales, only it broke up.'

'They always do.'

Tessie glared at her. 'I don't know why you have to be cynical. I think it's good, trying to set up an alternative way of life.'

'What, cooking rabbit stew, washing your clothes in a pond? You wouldn't last a week.'

Tessie tried to look disgusted but she couldn't keep a straight face. 'Anyway, the reason Billy knew Esme so well, he was one of the ones who tried to stop the new hypermarket being built.'

'Esme Fitch was in on that too?'

'It was her idea in the first place. She organised all the protests and even climbed a tree and stayed up it half the night.'

Karen nodded at the woman in green dungarees, who she was certain had once helped out in her mother's gift shop. Her mother had dozens of acquaintances but only a handful of close friends. As for her father, he didn't seem to have any real friends apart from the new girlfriend, who Karen wasn't even allowed to meet, and people he had known when he was still in the police. She had asked him if he knew Josh Bowen's father. *Mike Bowen, is it? Transferred to the area quite recently? Heard the name but, as far as I can remember I've never come across him.*

Tessie was still talking about the new hypermarket and how wicked it had been to destroy four chestnut trees.

'Yes, I suppose you're right. Listen, you know Esme Fitch asked if you thought she should go to the police . . . ?'

'She didn't say that exactly.' Tessie looked a little wary.

'What else did she say? Did she tell you—'

'Actually, I wasn't really concentrating all that well. I told you how she often complained about the police and how they were too heavy-handed.'

'Yes, but she might have discovered something important, something someone didn't want her to know. Oh, never mind.' It was obvious Tessie knew nothing about it. 'Josh Bowen, in the year above us at school.'

'Who?'

'You remember. He won the chess competition. D'you know anything about him?'

'What does he look like?'

Karen paused, wondering how best to describe him. 'Not very tall, serious-looking, brown hair, dark eyes. I saw him in the supermarket.'

'Is that all? Nice, is he?'

Karen shrugged. She had intended to tell Tessie about the shop-lifting. Suddenly she changed her mind. 'It's just – my father was asking if we knew him. His father's a police inspector, they only moved here a few months ago.'

\* \* \*

Alex's African violets looked distinctly unwell. Had she watered them too much or not enough, or were they coming to the end of their natural span?

The house felt strange with no-one around and just for a moment Karen sensed how it must feel to live alone. She thought about Esme Fitch. What had she been doing when the intruder broke in? Her father said time of death had been estimated at between eleven o'clock and one in the morning. Most likely she had gone to bed, then woken when she heard a noise. The police advised people to keep quiet, let the burglar take whatever he could find, then dial 999, but from everything she had heard about Miss Fitch it seemed likely she would have come downstairs, probably carrying some heavy object. Then Karen remembered it was a bungalow. Could anyone really stay in their bedroom, knowing there was someone in the next room who might turn the door handle at any minute?

A sudden noise made Karen jump, but it was only the postman. No, not the post, just someone delivering leaflets, inviting the occupant to phone now for a special offer on conservatories. Karen crumpled it into a ball, then remembered Alex's fantasies about sipping cocktails in the sun lounge and smoothed it out again.

After checking the back door and all the windows she left the house, turned the key in the mortise-lock, and pushing it into the top pocket in her jeans set off in the direction of the river. She had been hoping Tessie would accompany her to the Kite Festival, but naturally she was far too busy. It was getting on Karen's nerves the way all Tessie's time seemed to be taken up with the stupid petition, although, on second thoughts, perhaps it wasn't so much the petition itself as the fact that it gave her a chance to spend time with Billy Henderson. The way she had been gazing at him was nauseating. Half the time when Karen spoke to her she wasn't even listening. No wonder she had decided not to mention Josh Bowen and the shop-lifting.

She thought about the street map she had extracted from the bin outside the newsagent's. Esme Fitch's bungalow wasn't in Riverdale Road itself, and the cul-de-sac leading off it was so small it was almost impossible to read the name. Silvester Way had been abbreviated to Silvr. Way, and Josh's cross – she was assuming Josh had put it there – was large and smeary, and covered three or four side roads as well as part of Riverdale Road itself. Of course, it could refer to something quite different: a friend from school, although according to Mark Hill he had no friends; a house belonging to another chess enthusiast? If Josh had wanted to get rid of incriminating evidence why would he have thrown it in a public litter bin in the town centre? Then Karen remembered her father telling her that often the best way to hide something was to put it in a really obvious place.

Earlier in the day, when she had asked him about the Esme Fitch case, all he could come up with was the usual story that gets handed out to the press. The police were following up several leads and had interviewed several known burglars, but so far nothing of any consequence had turned up, neither was there any information from witnesses or from the forensic lab.

The sky was full of kites, but unless you were actually flying one yourself they didn't keep your attention for very long. The best one was in the shape of two fat legs and a pair of pink knickers. And there was another quite good one, a gigantic blue whale. Then a jokey voice, distorted by the wind and the tannoy system, announced that all single line fliers, or some such expression, must make way for the super-duper double line acrobatics.

Karen stayed a few moments longer, then crossed over the water meadows and started walking along the canal bank. The wind was blowing from the west, which always meant a foul smell from the factory that burned offal and old animal carcases. She covered her nose and mouth with her hand, turning her head now and again to watch the kites swoop close to the ground, then tear back up into the sky. A hundred metres ahead a man dressed in a long dark raincoat, with a bottle in his hand, was lurching from one side of the path to the other. Karen held her breath, praying he wouldn't fall in the canal so she would be obliged to try and fish him out. Then she saw

Josh. He was some distance ahead, but as she turned the corner there was no mistaking the hunched shoulders and faded green army jacket. Seeing him again so soon made Karen wonder whether he could have been following *her*. Perhaps he knew she had witnessed the shoplifting and was wondering what she intended to do about it. But surely not. If he was worried he could have spoken to her at the shopping centre.

What was it her father had told her about following suspects? Wear a reversible coat; that way, when no-one's looking you can turn it inside out and make yourself look like someone totally different. Reversing her sweatshirt wasn't going to be a lot of use. Besides, she was almost certain Josh had no idea she was interested in him. He was halfway over the bridge near the incinerator and she thought he was going to leave the canal, but he had only crossed to the other bank. If she continued on the same side would it be easy to keep him in sight, or did the opposite path go away from the water?

When she reached the pumping station he had

disappeared behind some trees. Then she noticed an old barge moored next to two wooden posts. It had curtains in one of the tiny windows but it looked in such a bad condition that she couldn't imagine anyone living on it, although these days people turned the most unpromising places into temporary homes. Her father had told her about a woman with a two-year-old child who had been found camping in a disused factory on the industrial estate.

Standing quite still, with a large chestnut tree between her and the canal, she thought she caught a glimpse of something moving inside the barge, but it could have been the reflection of a branch blowing in the wind. A duck was standing on a submerged piece of wood, or a large stone, so that only its feet were under the water. It was brown and white, half mallard, half farm duck. Did they interbreed or . . . ? A head had appeared from under the torn tarpaulin draped over the area outside the cabin. It was Josh.

Karen kept quite still, afraid that in the silence he would pick up the slightest sound. He paused for a moment, looking all around him, then climbed on to the edge of the barge, jumped on to the towpath, and squeezed through the hedge. Running flat out to a bridge she could see him in the distance, then returning along the other side of the canal she was just in time to see him reach the far end of a large field, then go through an open gate.

It was relatively easy to follow him. Keeping the same pace, but staying at least fifty metres behind, she watched him cross the main road without looking, so that a driver hooted angrily, then start up the hill. He never turned round, just kept going with his head well down and his shoulders hunched. He was walking quite fast and, since one of Karen's shoes had started rubbing her heel, she was glad when the road flattened out. After about a mile Josh stopped, stood staring into the distance for a few moments, then climbed a gate and sat on top of it, swinging his legs.

She slowed down, not wanting to get too close, but almost immediately he jumped off the gate and she saw his head bobbing above the hedge as he started walking along the edge of the field.

Now what? A short distance up the road she could see farm buildings – a barn, several ugly concrete outhouses, a tall silo – and in a short time she and Josh would both reach them, she on the road, he skulking behind the hedge.

Ewebank Farm. The first time she read it she pronounced it in her head as 'Ee-wee-bank', then realised her mistake and smiled. Ewe-bank. Sheepbank. But she couldn't see any sheep. At the far end of the yard a bald-headed man was sitting on a tractor, shouting to someone out of sight. 'I've told you a thousand times, not in there with the feed sacks.' Then a door clanged shut, and inside the house a phone started ringing.

'Can I help?' The voice came from only a couple of metres away and when Karen turned round she came face to face with a woman with her hand on the collar of a black-and-white sheepdog.

'Oh! No, thank you, I was just going for a walk.'

The woman eyed her suspiciously. 'Live in the village, do you?'

Karen shook her head. 'No, I've never been

here before. I didn't realise there was a farm so near the edge of the town.'

The woman looked at her as if she thought she was mad, then jerked her head towards the dog. 'If he'd bit you you'd only have had yourself to blame.'

Karen opened her mouth to say she had a perfect right to walk past, then remembered how she had been staring into the yard and decided against it. Moving away, not so fast that the woman would think she was afraid, but quick enough to make sure the dog was satisfied that its territory had not been invaded, she kept her eyes focused on the distant fields.

If Josh had gone round the back of the farm he would reappear sooner or later, unless he was hiding out somewhere. She walked up a steep lane on the opposite side to the farm, but after ten minutes or so of scanning the surrounding landscape and seeing only a few crows and wood pigeons, she realised she was wasting her time and decided to start back towards the town.

What had she learned about Josh? Nothing,

apart from the fact that he liked investigating old barges and creeping round the edges of farms. If he had made no friends since moving to the town maybe that was the only way he knew of passing the time. When he was at home, did he play chess against himself on his computer? Perhaps he missed his brother, but if he was so good at chess surely that meant he was pretty bright and Mark Hill's theory that he had failed the entrance exam to a boarding school couldn't be right. Of course, he might have been thrown out for stealing, or because of his disruptive behaviour, but that didn't seem likely either. As far as she knew he had never been in any trouble during his first term at their school, and if there had been any incidents Mark Hill would have been only too happy to tell her about it. There was something about Josh's sad, serious face and those dark, mournful eyes that made her feel sorry for him. He was lonely, an isolated newcomer who had been forced to change schools and disliked having to make new friends. But what about the shop-lifting and, far more important, the cross on the map? Did he really need her sympathy, or was there something sinister going on? Either way she was determined to find out more.

# Three

The funny smell had got worse during the last two days and the water took an age to run down the plug hole. Karen had broached the subject as tactfully as possible and now, at last, her father was on his knees, trying to unscrew the waste pipe. Perhaps it hadn't been the best time to ask him about the second victim of a supposed burglary, and whether she was still in intensive care.

'No, I told you,' he said irritably, 'they were worried about her breathing but in the end it turned out she was just badly shaken, plus a few cuts and bruises.'

'She was older than Esme Fitch?'

'Seventy-four and almost blind so she won't

41

be able to provide a description of the intruder, although it's possible he was spotted by a neighbour. A man whose baby wouldn't stop crying was wheeling it round in the dark, and claims to have seen someone with longish hair, dressed in some kind of flak jacket.' He straightened up, pressing his hand to his forehead. 'I'll phone for a plumber. Not this morning, I have to go out in ten minutes.'

Karen went to fetch some paracetamol. When she returned from the other room her father was slumped in a chair with his eyes closed.

'Had anything been taken from the house?' she asked.

'What? I believe a few trinkets may have gone missing, but nothing of any great value. By the way, that Bowen chap you mentioned is working on both cases.'

'You're sure?'

'Yes, of course I'm sure.' His eyes were still shut but he had picked up her increased curiosity. 'Why all the interest? You've taken a liking to the Bowen boy, have you?'

'No, nothing like that. I just wondered if the police think the same person did both break-ins.'

Her father accepted the two tablets and glass of water. 'Could have, I suppose. Your average burglar will do anything to avoid using violence.'

'Whereas this one's a real sadist.'

'That what you think, Karen?' He had one of his most patronising smiles. 'Sadist: a person who inflicts pain for the pleasure of it. If you want my opinion the second crime was committed by someone different. After all, if you'd accidentally killed a woman would you break into another house in the same part of town less than a week later?'

'Not unless it wasn't an accident, and the killer had a particular reason for killing Esme Fitch but wanted the police to think it was a burglary gone wrong.'

'Oh yes, and why would someone want to murder Miss Fitch? Because she sat up a tree, trying to prevent the contractors starting work on the new supermarket? Look, I hope you're not thinking of poking about, asking questions. You do have a tendency to let your imagination run away with you. By the way, have you watered your mother's plants? Which day is it they're coming home?'

'Looking forward to getting rid of me?' Karen was determined not to let him change the subject. 'D'you know where she lived, this second woman?'

'Why d'you want to know?' He handed her the empty glass. 'That road that runs up to the art college. Her name's Davis, Mary Davis, and you haven't answered my question about when your mother's coming back from France.'

Mrs Livingstone was pulling up weeds. Even in her gardening clothes she still managed to look like a housewife in a television commercial. When she saw Karen she stood up, rubbing the back of her shoulder, and indicated that they should sit down.

'Tessie's out, I'm afraid.'

'Collecting more signatures?'

Mrs Livingstone gave her a long, hard look.

'Am I to take it you don't entirely approve?'

Karen opened out a garden chair and sat down, hoping she had fixed it correctly and it wouldn't collapse under her. 'No, it's not that, I just think there's more important things to worry about.'

She expected a polite lecture on how, if we didn't respect the rights of animals we were unlikely to create a better world for human beings, but instead Mrs Livingstone started talking about Esme Fitch.

'Poor old thing, she was a born protester. I expect a psychologist would say she was working out her frustrations, but I'm sure we all have mixed motives for the things we do. Like Tessie; she just feels passionately about some things.'

'Have you heard anything?' Karen had decided not to mention the attack on Mary Davis. Tessie's mother didn't seem to have heard about it and she preferred to encourage her to carry on talking about Miss Fitch. 'Apparently the police have interviewed a few known burglars but nothing's come of it. I expect they're relying on an informer coming forward.'

Mrs Livingstone was leaning back in her striped deckchair. She looked tired but, with three children and a large house and garden to look after, that was hardly surprising. 'You know, Esme was frailer than she looked,' she said. 'She hated people to know her real age, liked to pretend she was at least ten years younger, but just recently she hadn't been all that well. She'd been seeing a chiropractor about her back, and a homeopath for her insomnia.'

'Homeopaths can cure insomnia?'

'Someone called Lydia Parfrey. Esme thought very highly of her, recommended her to all her friends and brought her several new clients. Then something happened.'

Karen was intrigued. 'What kind of something?'

'I've no idea. Esme was sweet, ready to drop everything if someone needed help, but she did rather tend to go from one extreme to the other. The doctor, the vicar, they were quite wonderful or they were perfectly useless. D'you know what I mean?'

Karen nodded. 'Tessie said she had strong opinions on most things. So you think this Lydia Parfrey may have fallen out of favour?'

'I'm not sure. Perhaps I got it all wrong. Anyway, the last time I saw Esme she talked of nothing but the way some pigs at a local farm were being kept. Tessie's father says pigs are quite happy indoors, provided their quarters are kept at the right temperature, but Esme would have none of it and I got the impression she and Ray Chapman had had a real ding-dong.'

'Chapman? That's the name of the farmer?' Karen tried to sound as casual as possible. 'I don't suppose you know the name of his farm, do you?'

'Something to do with sheep. Odd when it's a pig farm, but I daresay they changed, decided pigs were more profitable. He and Tessie's father are both members of a club that raises money for charity. We passed the farm once, not an attractive looking place, but they very rarely are these days with all those old tractor tyres and polythene bags. Oh, I remember. Ewebank.

47

Ewebank Farm. It's on the road that leads out towards the airport.'

Karen had expected Lydia Parfrey's consulting room to be in some kind of health centre, but the address turned out to be a private house in a small terrace not far from the cathedral. She rang the bell and waited, rehearsing her opening sentence over and over in her head. *Good morning, my name's Karen Cady and I'm doing a project on alternative forms of treatment. Good morning, my name's . . .*

'Hello.' A woman was coming up the street. She was about forty, very large, but the shape of her body was hidden beneath a loose-fitting orange-and-black dress that came almost to the ground. Her hair was thick and dark and she had a heavy fringe that stopped just above her eyebrows.

'I was looking for Lydia Parfrey,' said Karen.

'Then you've come to the right place.' Her voice was deep, almost like a man's. 'Did you want to make an appointment?'

Karen hesitated, not wanting to enter the

house under false pretences. 'It's just . . . I'm doing this school project on alternative medicine.'

'I see. And how did you know where I lived?'

'A Mrs Livingstone gave me your name. She was a friend of Esme Fitch.'

Lydia Parfrey stood quite still with her key in the lock. 'You knew Esme? I'm so sorry. What a dreadful thing to happen. I read about it in the local paper. It was the first I'd heard so it came as a terrible shock.'

She held open the door and invited Karen to go in ahead of her. 'First room on the left. Find somewhere to sit, I'll be back in a moment when I've fed the cat. I can spare half an hour, then I've a client booked in, I'm afraid.'

The room had three chairs, a large cupboard and a long couch like one in a doctor's surgery, except the couch looked rather old. The curtains were white with bunches of orange flowers, and the walls had been painted a kind of peach colour and had a frieze running around the top that was different from the curtains but obviously designed to go with them.

Karen sat down on the only hard chair, which somehow felt safer than sinking into one of the upholstered ones, and took a small pad from her pocket. Lydia Parfrey had assumed she knew Esme Fitch and it would be best to leave it that way. Once she had asked a few questions about homeopathy she would mention Miss Fitch again and see how she reacted.

She could hear sounds coming from the kitchen at the back of the house, cupboards opening and closing, the clatter of knives and forks. While she waited she thought about Miss Fitch and wondered if she had sat on the same chair she was sitting on now, or had she lain on the couch and talked about her childhood and all those years she had lived at Stockwood House? Then she thought about Josh, and Ewebank Farm, and the way Miss Fitch had rowed with the farmer. Had the man she had seen on the tractor been Ray Chapman?

When Lydia Parfrey returned she had combed her hair and was wearing a pair of dangling earrings shaped like crescent moons, which Karen was sure she hadn't had on before.

'Now, how can I help? Your project's not just about homeopathy?'

'No, all kinds of alternative treatments.' Karen started to reel off the list she had prepared but Mrs Parfrey held up her hand.

'I tell you what, I'll describe the basic principles of homeopathy and give you an idea of the kind of things I do, then if you have any questions . . .' She glanced at a clock on the mantelpiece. 'And before you leave remind me to give you a leaflet that you might find quite useful.'

She talked very fast and with enormous enthusiasm, describing how she had only qualified a year ago and her practice had only been going for about four months. 'It took time to find the right premises, not so far away from the city centre that those without a car would have difficulty reaching me, but of course it had to be in a relatively quiet street. I think this fits the bill rather well.'

Karen made notes on her pad. Time was running out. If Lydia Parfrey didn't stop talking soon her client would arrive and there would be no chance to ask any questions.

'Esme told me you'd helped her a lot,' she said, interrupting Lydia's account of how the mind and the body had to be treated as a whole. 'She was always recommending you to people.'

'That was kind.'

'I felt really sorry for her. Before she moved to the bungalow she used to live in Stockwood House, only it had to be sold when her parents died.'

Mrs Parfrey was staring at her. 'I didn't realise you knew Miss Fitch so well. You say a Mrs Livingstone gave you my name?'

Karen swallowed. 'Yes, that's right. She's the mother of one of my friends from school. Esme used to talk about someone called Lydia, but I always thought you were a doctor.'

'I see.' She was staring at Karen, her expression fixed in an unnatural smile. 'From everything she told me I got the impression she'd never got over having to leave the family home. Apparently it was sold to a retired general, then it passed to his son.'

'And now Peter Quayle has brought it,' said Karen brightly. 'You know, I was wondering, if someone gets really upset and angry can it make them physically ill?'

Lydia Parfrey looked at the clock, then back at Karen. 'Of course, that's what I've been trying to explain. The fact that someone else was living in "her" house could well have been the root cause of most of Miss Fitch's aches and pains.'

She sounded edgy. She obviously wanted Karen to leave. Sitting there, with her arms folded across her chest, she looked rather like the teacher who had taught them Biology in the first year, and reduced several people, including one of the boys, to tears.

'Anyway,' Karen scribbled some more notes, 'thank you very much for sparing the time.'

'My pleasure.' Lydia stood up, then turned towards the window. 'If they demolished the old warehouses I'd have quite a view from here. Esme had strong feelings about the environment. I expect she talked to you about her political activities.'

'You mean the demonstration she organised to try and stop them building the new hypermarket? She could be quite outspoken, couldn't she? I expect she sometimes upset people, without meaning to, of course.'

Lydia Parfrey smiled. 'She was a lovely person, I was fond of her, but she did tend to let her imagination run away with her.'

'Yes, I know what you mean.' With a little more encouragement she might persuade her to say a bit more. 'I think she had quite a few enemies, as well as a lot of friends, of course.'

Lydia gave a little self-conscious laugh. 'Oh, surely *enemies* is putting it much too strongly. Did she tell you she was on the track of a car thief?'

'Car thief?' Was this a way of checking if Karen had really known Esme Fitch as well as she was making out?

'I never grasped exactly what she was on about. Of course, she often talked about how cars ought to be banned from the city centre, but when I asked her to tell me more she just made some joke about a gooseberry bush. Poor old thing, I think her mind had started to wander just a tiny bit. One moment it was as sharp as can be, the next . . .' She was moving towards the door. 'Anyway, good luck with your project, and if there's anything else you need to know don't hesitate to give me a ring.'

# *Four*

Why had she volunteered to help? Because she didn't like the way Tessie was acting, as if she had a monopoly on good deeds? Whatever the reason it certainly had nothing to do with Billy Henderson. She had had no idea he was going to be one of the group assembled outside the entrance to the playing fields. They were all there to help extend the footpath so it was possible to walk along the river without having to make a detour through part of a housing estate. The project was being organised by the Nature Trust and, since most of the work involved cutting back the undergrowth, they had been advised to wear clothes that would protect them from the nettles and brambles.

Billy was wearing the same black trousers, but his hooded sweatshirt had been replaced by a crumpled tee shirt with a rip under one arm. When Karen joined the group he frowned, trying to remember.

'Karen,' she said, 'I'm a friend of Tessie's.'

'Yes, of course. Didn't know you were in on this lark.' He spread his arms, indicating the mass of tangled branches.

'It seemed like a good idea,' she said. 'The footpath, I mean.'

'Let's hope so, although I wouldn't use it after dark if I were you. They say someone was mugged a bit further along.'

'That was ages ago.'

'You heard about it then? Of course, your father's a private eye, like in the movies, eh?'

The group leader had arrived and was making signals for everyone to move closer. Billy gave Karen an amused look, through half-closed eyes. 'Don't worry, I'm not that stupid. Beats doing a real job though. Doesn't need an assistant, does he?'

For the next two hours they hardly spoke to

each other. The work was hard and several times Karen found herself wondering why she had agreed to take part. Now that she had been once it wouldn't stop there. Her name would be on some list and she would receive endless requests to fill potholes or clear out evil-smelling ponds.

In spite of the fact that there was plenty to be done, time dragged and she kept looking up at the sky, hoping for a downpour that would put an end to the afternoon session. She met a girl called Vicky who had been in her class at primary school and they exchanged a few words, but they had never been close friends. Eventually the team leader announced that it was time to pack up, but he hoped everyone would be back at the weekend to carry on the good work. Karen wouldn't. Glancing briefly at Billy, who was talking to a girl wearing a red baseball cap, she picked up her jacket and started walking back towards the main road.

While she was hacking at the undergrowth she had attempted to sort out her thoughts – about Esme Fitch, and the second attack on Mary Davis – but there had been too much noise; people shouting to each other, two boys singing the same song over and over again at the top of their voices. There were so many unanswered questions. Had Esme Fitch tried to create so much trouble about the way the pigs were kept that the farmer had called round at her house to give her a verbal warning that had turned into something much worse? Then there was her remark to Lydia Parfrey about a car thief. Was catching joy-riders another of her crusades?

And what about Josh Bowen? Had he anything at all to do with it? It occurred to Karen that he might know if Esme Fitch had threatened the owner of Ewebank Farm? Was he as interested as she was to find out who had killed her? Her suspicions about him might have been quite misplaced. In fact, it was possible he knew a good deal more about the case than she did. But, apart from her, everyone seemed to accept that Miss Fitch's death had been a tragic accident. After all, she had no real evidence it was anything else, just a gut feeling, and she knew what her father thought about gut feelings. Mrs Livingstone had described Esme Fitch as 'a dear', but the more

Karen learned about her the more she realised Tessie's mother had probably been indulging in her usual practice of seeing the best in people . . .

A hand came down on her shoulder. Billy Henderson had caught up with her and was asking which way she was going.

She hesitated, then pointed in the direction of the town centre.

'Me too, mind if I tag along? I was thinking . . . your father's job must be fascinating. Do you hear about all the latest cases?'

'How do you know what his job is? I suppose Tessie must have told you.'

Billy frowned. 'She may have mentioned it. Actually, I don't know Tessie all that well. I've been away from the area for a year or so, at college. Stuck it for a couple of terms but it didn't work out.'

'So you joined a community in Wales, only that didn't work out either.'

He laughed. 'OK, so we both know the basics about each other. Anyway, how's the petition going? Been helping Tessie collect more signatures?'

'No, I haven't had the time.' Why did she sound so defensive? But that was the way people involved in protest movements always made you feel.

Billy smiled. 'Trouble with good causes is they provide a perfect opportunity for people to get rid of their pent-up aggression in what appears to be a socially acceptable way. That fat bloke you saw me with, calls himself Craig but that's really his surname. Still with a first name like Francis who can blame him?'

'What about him?'

'Turns up at all the demonstrations, but I doubt if he even knows what most of them are about.'

'What about the girl with beads in her hair?'

'Selina? Oh, Selina's a nutcase. Didn't Tessie tell you?' He took hold of her arm at the elbow. 'Come on, we'll cross here, it's hopeless further up.'

Halfway across the road Karen thought she heard him mention Esme Fitch, but a bus had pulled up with its engine running noisily and she only caught the last few words.

'Another old person's been beaten up,' she said, hoping he would repeat what he had just said.

He nodded. 'That weird-looking house up near the art college. Look, I'm sorry, I haven't been completely straight with you. My father once used the services of the Cady Detective Agency. He owns an electronics business. There was some trouble with one of his employees a couple of years back and he needed her checked out. By the way, you didn't answer my question.'

'What question?'

'When we were crossing the road. D'you think it's possible Esme Fitch was much better off than anyone thought? I mean, the way she talked I got the impression she had trouble making ends meet, but surely her parents must have left her a good whack of cash.'

'You mean because they lived in Stockwood House?' she asked. 'But after they died she had to sell up.'

'Oh, sure, but those kind of people are never left penniless. Oh well, it was just a thought. Old people can do funny things, not that there was anything wrong with Esme's brain, but she had some fairly strong opinions about bank managers. I wondered if she could have been the kind who kept her cash under the floorboards.'

'And someone found out, and decided to break into the bungalow?'

'Why not? But there wouldn't be any need to break in. Whoever it was could have called round selling conservatories or something, asked to have a look at the back, just to check, then forced their way into the kitchen.'

The way he was talking it was almost as if he knew. He noticed her expression and smiled.

'Just a thought. The only way to catch the guy is to try and put yourself in his position. If Esme'd been a bloke she'd have had a pub where she was a regular and someone could've checked up who she'd talked to, who could've known what was hidden in the bungalow.'

'But we don't even know there was anything.'

He ignored this. 'There's the art class, I suppose. Oh, what's the good, she could have told any number of people, which reminds me, have you ever come across someone called Lydia Parfrey?'

'Yes, she's the homeopath Esme Fitch used to see.'

'And Mary Davis, the latest victim. She saw the Parfrey woman too. You've met her, have you?'

'I've seen her.' She could hardly tell him she'd been round to the consulting room near the cathedral. 'Somebody once pointed her out. You know Mary Davis?'

He shook his head. 'Craig's mother went to school with her daughter. You know, the way Esme talked I was afraid she was going to end up in court. Not long before the break-in she was going all over the place, slagging off homeopathy and saying homeopaths took your money under false pretences.'

The pavement had narrowed so that soon there would be only room to walk in single file. Billy slowed down and stood close to the wall to let Karen go ahead.

'If you ask me,' he said, 'the poor woman suggested, as diplomatically as possible, that some of Esme's symptoms might be up here.'

He tapped the side of his head. 'That would've been quite enough to do the trick.'

'I thought you liked Esme.'

'Oh, I did.' The traffic was roaring past and it was quite difficult to hear what he was saying. 'As long as you kept on the right side of her she was great. Need more people like Esme, most people are so boring, so careful of what they say or do. Trouble was she always went just that little bit too far. It wasn't enough to fall out with Lydia Parfrey, she had to go round telling everyone the woman was a charlatan and they had better stay clear of her if they wanted to protect their sanity.'

She had told her father she was going for a walk and he had nodded, without taking his eyes off the computer screen.

'Is there anything to eat?'

'Yes, of course. I'll be back in about an hour. We're having pizza and don't worry, there isn't any pepperoni.'

She turned into Barton Gardens, then took the short cut that led through to Victoria Park.

A weird house at the end of Chesterfield Road. Karen had no idea what Billy had meant, but since she didn't know the number of the house she hoped it would be obvious. She could see the roofs of the art college and it reminded her how Mrs Livingstone and Esme Fitch had attended the same class, although that had been held at the Adult Education Centre. Tessie had told her how most of the members returned year after year. Did people think Esme's paintings were any good? Tessie wasn't sure. *You saw the picture of a naked woman. Most of them seem to do watercolours, but Esme liked oil paint because she said you could apply it with a palette knife in great dollops.*

As far as Karen could tell everything Esme Fitch had done had been in great dollops. She wished they had met.

The weird house came into view. There was no mistaking it. Part of it was single storey, with a flat roof, but the rest was on two floors, although the upstairs rooms had very small windows. The house had been painted pink, with a pale blue front door, and a roughly-made porch that had an assortment of shells pressed into the concrete. The whole place stood out from the rest of the street, like a gingerbread house in a children's book. Along the left-hand side a lean-to greenhouse ran from front to back, and Karen could see it contained a large number of drooping tomato plants. Would somebody water them while Mrs Davis was in hospital? Did she have friendly neighbours or was she the kind of person who kept herself to herself? Karen's father had told her Mary Davis was a widow who had lived on her own since her husband's death more than ten years ago. She had three children, but none of them lived close by and, as far as the police could tell, they only visited her at Christmas.

Karen walked straight past, pretending she was on her way to somewhere quite different, then turned the corner and came back along the narrow alleyway that ran behind all the houses. The path was cleaner than she expected; no heaps of litter that had spilled out when the dustmen came to empty the bins, just a few empty paint tins and the remains of a bike that had been stripped of its wheels. The houses were detached and it was possible to see over most of the garden walls. Mary Davis's house was the third from the end. The garden looked rather overgrown but it was the sort Karen liked, far better than the way her mother – no, it was Alex's idea – had managed to create something that would have looked overdone at the Chelsea Flower Show.

Placing her foot in the hole left by a missing brick, she hoisted herself up to get a better view. The back of the house had a veranda, with a basket rocking-chair, like in an American film set in the Deep South. A climbing plant obscured part of a large window. Two other, smaller, windows had their curtains drawn.

A bush to the right of the porch was covered in berries, some of which had dropped to the ground, and behind it she could see a tall laburnum with its long, dangling, poisonous flowers. A sudden movement caught her eye. Something, a fox, or even a badger, was pushing its way through the undergrowth. A few small birds rose in the air, then the creature appeared, only it wasn't a fox.

Still on all fours Josh Bowen crept towards the

veranda, keeping his head well down but moving it from side to side as if he was searching for something.

As Karen watched he seemed to be scratching at the dry earth with his nails. Then she heard him let out a small gasp, and a moment later he stood up, holding something in his hand. Whatever it was, it was something small. A button? A coin? He tilted back his head, almost like a dog sniffing the air, remained quite still for a few moments, then suddenly darted round the side of the house.

Dashing back along the alleyway she was just in time to see him turn right at the opposite end of the road and disappear out of sight.

## *Five*

It would be unfair to tell anyone about Josh without giving him a chance to explain. First the map with Riverdale Road marked with a cross, now the incident in Mary Davis's garden. Compared with these two things, the shop-lifting and the walk round Ewebank Farm seemed insignificant. Was it really possible that Josh had robbed Mary Davis, then realised he had dropped some incriminating evidence and gone back to retrieve it? And what about Esme Fitch? The post-mortem had revealed that she had died of a cerebral haemorrhage that could have been caused by a blow to the head, but could equally well have been the result of her hitting her head when she fell. It was difficult to believe that Josh could be connected in any way with such a serious crime, or was it just that she didn't want to believe it?

She was in the city centre, doing the weekend shopping. If she was honest with herself she had to admit it would be quite a relief when her mother and Alex returned and she could forget about supplies of milk, breakfast cereal, honey, apples . . . Her father bought takeaways two or three times a week. She would miss the chicken chow mein, fish in soggy batter, and tepid curry, but she would have no regrets about giving up cooking the meals they ate on the remaining days.

Hoisting the three carrier bags into a more comfortable position, she watched a large white car turn at the lights, then slowly worm its way past the taxi rank and on through the part where the road narrowed and the pavement widened.

'It's that bloke,' said a voice behind her, and Karen turned her head to see if the voice was talking to her.

He wasn't, but she recognised him as one of the people who had been helping Tessie gather signatures for her petition.

'What bloke's that?' asked his friend.

The first man jerked his head towards the white vehicle. 'Peter Quayle. Lives in that big place out in the country. He was on the telly shooting his mouth off about the free market and the need for proper rewards for people prepared to plough profits back into their businesses.'

'Oh, him.' The second man was scornful. 'Not difficult to see where his profits have gone. A Shogun, I ask you, what's the point of a four-wheel-drive off-roader in a busy city centre.'

The car had pulled up on the double yellow lines. A woman in the passenger seat jumped out, laughing as she caught her shoe on the edge of the pavement and nearly fell headlong.

Peter Quayle raised his hand in a wave, leaned across to slam the passenger door, then moved slowly off in the direction of the roundabout.

It all happened so quickly. One minute Karen was watching the car, the next she saw Josh standing a hundred metres away on the opposite side of the road. In that split second she realised he knew who she was. Then, to her horror, he made a sudden dash. There was nothing Peter Quayle could have done to avoid him. The Shogun swerved, looked for a moment as if it might even turn on its side, then skidded to a halt just a few metres beyond where Josh was lying in the gutter.

Karen ran faster than she had ever run in her life. 'Josh! Josh, are you all right?' There was no blood, or if there was the injury was not visible. His straggly hair had fallen across his face. She wanted to smooth it back, but she was afraid to touch him. Someone had gone into a shop to phone for an ambulance, then a woman who claimed to have a knowledge of first aid stepped forward and knelt beside Josh in the road.

'Mustn't move him, love,' she said, believing that since Karen knew his name she must be a close friend or relative. 'Ambulance will be here in a sec.'

Peter Quayle had joined them. Even if Karen hadn't seen him a few minutes before she would have recognised him from his photos in the paper, and his television appearances. His face looked pale grey and the hand that came out to touch Josh's arm was shaking.

'God, is he all right?'

'Wasn't your fault, love,' said the woman. 'I saw the whole thing. He never looked, just ran straight across.'

'He's breathing?'

She nodded reassuringly. 'Just a few bruises, I expect. They'll take X-rays to make sure.' She put her face very near to Josh. 'That's it, love, you keep quite still. Ambulance will be here any minute, there's a good lad.'

Peter Quayle accompanied Josh in the ambulance. So did Karen. Like the woman in the street, the ambulance men had assumed she was a friend and told her to hop in. As they drove off she could see the white Shogun, half on the road, half on the pavement, then she heard Quayle introducing himself and turned to see him holding out his hand.

'Karen,' she said, 'Karen Cady. I go to the same school as Josh.'

He nodded. His suntan contrasted with the short hair she had always thought of as blond, but which she could now see was grey, almost white. He was in his early thirties, she remembered that much, and he prided himself on his casual appearance. Jeans, denim jacket, open-necked shirt; they set him apart, made him different from the usual self-made millionaire, not that Karen had ever met a millionaire before and, come to think of it, these days you probably had to make at least ten to qualify as a real success.

She expected him to launch into an explanation of how there had been nothing he could do, how, without warning, Josh had just run out into the road, but instead he asked if the two of them knew each other well.

'No, hardly at all,' she said. 'He only moved to the area a few months ago.'

'Where does he live?'

'I'm sorry.' She felt a bit of an idiot. 'I don't even know that, I mean, I don't really know anything about him.'

'Not true,' said a voice, and the two of them turned towards the stretcher where Josh was lying on his back with his eyes closed, covered in a red blanket.

Josh was kept in hospital for observation. He was suffering from concussion and had a badly-broken arm, but he was going to be all right. Karen felt sick with relief. She blamed herself for what had happened. He knew she had been following him, checking up on him, and when he saw her again he had panicked, dashing across the road without thinking. He could have been seriously injured. He could have been killed.

Peter Quayle gave her a lift back to the shopping centre in his taxi. While they were still at the hospital he had insisted on phoning her father, but had only got through to the answering machine: 'Cady's Detective Agency. If you'd like to leave a message someone will get back to you as soon as possible.' At the time he had made no comment. Now, sitting in the back of the taxi, he started asking one question after another.

'Your father's a private detective? His own business is it? How did he get started?'

'He was in the police.'

'Yes, I see. So he has all the right contacts.'

Although his hair was grey, his eyebrows were

quite dark, but she had seen people like that before although they were usually a good deal older. The casual clothes were a way of demonstrating that it was possible to get rich without wearing a boring suit and a tie. Karen remembered reading that he had left school at sixteen, found a job stacking shelves in a supermarket, then worked his way up at lightning speed until he had enough experience, and money, to start his own company, selling some wonder product that, if you ate it regularly, 'kept your body in balance'. She remembered Alex talking about it and her mother, who would once have poured scorn on such a product, saying it was certainly worth a try.

Quayle was watching her intently. 'What happened to your shopping?' he asked, and she put her hand up to her mouth, realising that she must have left it at the hospital.

'It doesn't matter,' she said. 'Anyway, it's not worth going back for.'

'Sure?' He smiled at her and she felt a little weak, which was hardly surprising. When they were leaving one of the nurses had asked her how she was getting home and, when she told her she was going in Mr Quayle's taxi, he had immediately insisted she call him Peter.

There was something about him. He was the kind of person people want to be with, the kind who turns a boring get-together into something interesting, exciting. In spite of the accident – or perhaps it was because he felt the same relief she did that Josh had not been badly hurt – he looked relaxed, but also gave the impression he was bursting with energy. He talked very fast, never about himself, always about Karen, or her father, or to ask if she liked her school and what her plans were for the future. He had a way of giving you his full, undivided attention. If his aim was to make you like him, it certainly worked.

The driver twisted round to ask where he should drop them off.

'Anywhere,' said Peter. 'Just over there will be fine.' He turned to Karen. 'Listen, I think I should take you home, talk to one of your parents, explain what happened.'

That was the last thing she wanted. 'There

won't be anyone there,' she said firmly. 'Anyway, there's no need.'

'Your father still won't be in his office?'

She shook her head. 'He's had to go out for the whole day.'

'Is there someone else then? He has a business partner?'

'Just the answering machine.'

Peter smiled. 'Well, at least let me buy you a cup of coffee.'

They were standing on the pavement, not far from where Josh had run across the road. Karen hesitated, part of her wanting to get away, be by herself, but another part . . .

'Oh, come on,' he said, 'it won't take long. I just want to make sure you're all right, no delayed after-effects.'

He chose a place she had never been to before, asked if she drank cappuccino, and returned a couple of minutes later with a cup piled high with froth and grated chocolate. His own cup was smaller and contained plain black coffee. They sat on high stools and he started telling her how he had recently taken up riding.

'Mainly as a way of seeing the countryside, not that there are all that many places left where it's safe to take a horse.'

'No.' Karen felt stupidly tongue-tied.

'You don't ride then?'

'No.'

'So what are your particular interests?' He sounded as if he really wanted to know, but of course it was just a practised technique, a way of making people feel special.

'I'd like to work with my father,' she said. 'Only it's not the kind of job you can do until you've had some other kinds of experience.'

'No, I can see that.' He finished his coffee, then caught the eye of a waitress and asked for a refill. 'But presumably it doesn't mean you'd actually have to join the police force first?'

She wanted to talk about Esme Fitch. There was no way of gradually introducing the subject so she would have to take a deep breath and ask him straight out. 'I expect you've heard about Miss Fitch?'

He broke off in mid-sentence. 'Yes, yes, of

course. It was a horrible thing to happen, I was very shocked.'

'Another woman's been attacked in her home,' she said. 'She's in hospital but she's not seriously injured, she's going to be all right.'

'Thank goodness for that. Your father's involved with the cases? Surely the police—'

'No, it's not that. Esme, Miss Fitch, she was a friend.'

'I'm sorry.' He sounded so genuinely sympathetic that Karen felt a twinge of guilt. 'As you probably know, I moved into Stockwood House fairly recently. Going back a few years, it was the Fitch family home, not that I ever actually met Miss Fitch but there are people in the village who remember her well.'

Karen sucked some of the froth off her cappuccino, hoping none of it had stuck to her mouth. 'I don't think Esme ever got over having to move into the bungalow.'

Peter frowned. 'I'm sorry about that, but she'd been living there quite a time though, hadn't she? There were two other owners of Stockwood before I bought the place.'

'Perhaps it would have been better if she'd moved right away from this area.'

'Perhaps.' He smiled and, to her annoyance, she could feel the colour rising in her face. She should have been thinking about poor Josh, lying in his hospital bed, but all she could think was how she was going to tell Tessie she had shared a taxi with Peter Quayle and, even better, he had bought her a coffee afterwards.

'I'm sure you don't need to worry about Josh,' he said, misinterpreting the expression on her face. 'I'll keep in touch, of course, but the doctor assured me he'll be home by the end of the week.'

Keep in touch? Then she realised he meant with the hospital.

'I might go and visit him tomorrow,' she said, hoping he would say he was going to do the same.

'Yes, I'm sure he'd appreciate that, although you say he's not a close friend, just someone you know from school.'

She wanted to tell him everything. How she had seen Josh shop-lifting; how, only a couple of days ago, he had been searching Mary Davis's garden and picked something up from the grass.

She had spoken to Josh at the hospital and been convinced that the desperation in his eyes had nothing to do with the accident. If she turned up at visiting time would he agree to see her, or would he make some excuse, saying he was too tired or felt too unwell? She would wait in the corridor outside the ward until a nurse persuaded him that he really ought to talk to her, even if it was for only a couple of minutes. She had to find out why he had run into the road. She had to know if it had been because of her.

# *Six*

Her father was working on two cases that kept him out of the office most of the day: a dodgy insurance claim, and a woman who wanted him to try and trace the sister she had lost touch with thirty years ago.

Karen thought about all the effort she had made to persuade him that she ought to come and live with him. Now, with her mother and Alex on holiday, her wish had come true, even if it was only for a couple of weeks, but things weren't turning out quite as she had expected. The flat was tiny and her father, who had never been a great conversationalist, liked to spend his evenings watching endless news bulletins and documentaries. When the television was switched off she tried to chat about this and that – Tessie's petition, the Nature Trust project to clear the footpath by the river, and so on – but his eyes usually started to glaze over and she would notice him having surreptitious looks at his watch.

Questions about Esme Fitch or Mary Davis met with even less response, although he had let drop the fact that the two of them had known each other slightly. *They both collected money for a sanctuary for horses. Old, clapped-out ones, I imagine. Never ceases to amaze me how people are more prepared to hand over money for animals than they are for their fellow human beings.* At the time Karen had considered making a comment about how the horses had probably been exploited and ill-treated by human beings, but she had thought better of it. She didn't want to turn into another Tessie.

She could hear his footsteps on the pavement outside the office window, and when he entered the flat she could tell at once that he was in a good mood.

'Everything all right?' he asked, dropping his briefcase on the floor, then pouring himself a drink. 'Any messages, anything urgent?'

She shook her head. 'A call from someone called Arthur but he said he'd ring back later.'

'The Esme Fitch case,' he announced. 'You'll be interested to know the police had Ray Chapman in for questioning. They'd heard a rumour that Miss Fitch had threatened to let his pigs loose, or even set fire to his barn, but he had a very convincing alibi for the night she was killed.'

'Where was he?'

'Oh, come on, Karen, they don't let me in on every detail. Now, what have you been doing today? Not sitting around indoors, I hope. Been hacking away at the brambles again?'

'Anyway,' she said, ignoring his question, 'people don't kill an old lady just because she's made some silly threats. Oh, I forgot to tell you before,' she filled the kettle, preparing to make his obligatory pot of tea, 'I met a friend of Tessie's and he says you know his father. He's called Billy Henderson.'

'Who is, the father or the son? Oh, you mean Derek Henderson. William calls himself Billy now, does he? Well, I suppose that's all part of the new image. Had a brilliant career ahead of him, then chucked in his degree course and joined some barmy cult in the wilds of west Wales.'

'Maybe it was more important to him,' she said, deliberately taking an opposing point of view, then smiling because they both knew what she was doing. 'Sorry, I think it was pretty stupid too.' She was building up to telling him about Josh Bowen's accident, but for some reason it was making her nervous. She could feel her heart beating in her chest. 'You remember I asked if you knew Inspector Bowen?'

'What about him? I've met him at last, but I can't say I took to him all that much.' He folded his arms. He had picked up her anxiety. He always did.

'His son was knocked down by a car. No, it's all right, it wasn't serious, but I was the only person who knew who he was so I went with him in the ambulance. Me and Peter Quayle.'

'Peter Quayle? What on earth were you doing with—'

'It was his car, only it wasn't his fault. Josh just ran into the road. Actually, he's quite nice. Peter Quayle is, I mean. Not at all what you'd expect, not really that arrogant or full of himself.'

'You obviously took rather a fancy to him. So the boy's going to be all right. In your class at school, is he?'

'No, I told you, he's a year ahead. I suppose I ought to go and see him some time. They're keeping him in hospital for a few days. His arm was broken in two places.'

'Good idea, I expect he'd appreciate a visit. Look, I've a few phone calls to make, then I'm afraid I have to go out again.'

'When?' For some reason Karen felt absurdly upset. 'Oh, you mean to see your girlfriend. I was wondering, has she got two heads or something? Is that why I never get to meet her?'

Her father opened his mouth but she didn't stay to hear what was coming next. As she ran down the steps to the street he called after her, probably to complain that she hadn't finished making the tea.

She started walking towards the river. She had

no idea where she was going or what she was going to do when she got there, but she wasn't hanging around any longer, just to be treated like some kind of slave.

The following day it poured with rain till lunchtime, then the sun came out, making the pavements steam. Karen had spent the morning cleaning the flat, ironing shirts, then tidying up the office. Her father was out again, but she didn't mind. One of the good things about him was that he never went in for boring post-mortems over minor events that were best forgotten. Her mother and Alex were always on about feelings. One or other of them would decide something had annoyed or upset her and, if she didn't manage to make a quick exit, the two of them would gaze at her understandingly and ask if she wanted to talk about how she felt.

Another postcard had arrived, from somewhere called Souillac, with a picture of some dreary old abbey and a note from Alex about how it had been rebuilt in the seventeenth century – as if she cared. Her mother had added a few words at the end, but they were almost impossible to read. *Hope you're eating properly*. Or was it *Hope you're watering the pelargonia* – or whatever her precious plant was called.

All morning she had been preparing for her visit to the hospital. Now, when she glanced at the clock, she realised if she didn't get a move on she was going to be late. Visiting hours were between two and four-thirty, but presumably Josh's parents were allowed to stay with him as long as they liked. If she turned up dead on two there was just a chance his mother would have gone to have her lunch. If not, she would give him the chocolates she had bought, chat if she got the chance, then leave after five minutes or so. Would he be expecting her? She had promised to come back but she wasn't even sure he had been listening.

As she was leaving the flat she remembered her father telling her he had run out of shampoo. Using hers was no good, he had to have his specially formulated anti-dandruff brand. The way he handed out orders it was difficult to understand how he had managed before she was around, or what he would do when she returned home.

Fighting her way past the shelves of 'easy-application natural tint hair colourants', she snatched up the shampoo and joined the shortest checkout queue, counting out change while idly watching the shoppers on the other side of the road. A familiar figure was coming out of the candle shop. This time her dress was calf-length and made out of some gauzy kind of material that had been tie-dyed in various shades of green, yellow and black. Pausing for a moment on the pavement, she opened a paper bag, lifted out something, removed the tissue paper it was wrapped in, and held it up to the light.

Karen left the chemist's and crossed over. Now was her chance. She might never have another.

'Mrs Parfrey?'

Lydia Parfrey jumped slightly, then her face lit up in a beaming, if slightly artificial, smile. 'Karen, I suppose we were bound to bump into each other sooner or later, although I never imagined it would be so soon. Look.' The candle in her hand was shaped like a yellow waterlily. 'Isn't it beautiful.'

'Yes, lovely.' Karen tried not to stare at the deep scratches on the back of both of Lydia's hands. Had they been there before? Maybe the cat had scratched her. She had no recollection of having noticed them, but neither could she remember the large, chunky rings. 'By the way, thank you for talking to me. It was really helpful.'

'Good, I'm glad.' She replaced the candle in its bag. 'I'm afraid it was all a bit of a rush. As I said, if you need any more information do give me a ring and we can fix a time when I'm not so busy. Perhaps when you've finished the project you might like me to take a quick look.'

'Yes. Thanks.' It was the last thing Karen wanted, but what could she say? She started to move away, but Lydia Parfrey called her back.

'Just one thing, Karen. Miss Fitch, Esme, I'm awfully afraid I may have given the wrong impression. As I said before, she was a dear, and very amusing. Just a little confused perhaps, but it's easily done when we're tired, overwrought. I'm sure we can all be the same.'

Karen smiled but said nothing, and this seemed to make Mrs Parfrey even more agitated. She was standing on one leg with the other foot pressed against the wall, and she kept pressing her lips together, like Mrs Livingstone did after she had applied her pale pink lipstick. Now she came to think of it, Lydia Parfrey wore a fair amount of make-up. The first time they met Karen had been so apprehensive she had tried not to meet Lydia's eyes more than was absolutely necessary. Now she could see they had black liner round them and her eyelashes were thick enough and long enough to be false.

'Anyway,' said Lydia, in a voice that was meant to sound cheery but only came out high-pitched and brittle, 'I didn't want you to think I was criticising. She was a friend of yours, you must be very upset.'

Later, when Karen went over the conversation in her head, it occurred to her that Lydia Parfrey had been making a huge effort to convince her that she had really liked Esme Fitch. Why had she got exactly the opposite impression?

\* \* \*

As it turned out she had no way of knowing whether Josh was surprised to see her or not. He was propped up in bed, with his arm in plaster from the wrist right up to the shoulder, and he had his eyes firmly focused on the wall opposite. The arm looked worse than she had expected, but it was the paleness of his face that really alarmed her.

'How are you?' she asked, sounding more relaxed than she felt. 'I just came to tell you how sorry I was.'

He said nothing, but she thought he looked slightly uneasy.

She tried again. 'Was it because you saw me, was that the reason you ran across the road?'

He stared at her. 'It was nothing to do with you. It was something I'd been planning for a long time.'

'I don't understand.' A nurse was approaching, but when she reached Josh all she did was smile, then start drawing a curtain round the patient in the next bed.

Karen studied the uneaten fruit on the locker beside Josh's bed. 'What d'you mean, you'd been planning it for a long time?' she said. 'You'll have to explain. I don't know anything about you, except that you won the chess competition at school.'

He sighed. 'Not many people went in for it.'

'And someone said you've got a brother at boarding school.'

He jerked forward, wincing with pain as he accidentally moved his arm. 'Who told you that?'

'I'm not sure,' she lied, then changed her mind. 'Oh, I know, it was Mark Hill. I remember because he mentioned how your father was a policeman and my father used to be in the police too.'

He nodded vaguely. 'Mr Quayle told me about your father being a private detective. What's his name?'

'Bob Cady. And mine's Karen.'

He closed his eyes and she wondered if he wanted to go to sleep. 'Why didn't you tell them?' he asked.

'Tell who?'

'After you saw me throw the map in the bin.'

How much did he know? Had he seen her

following him along the canal bank, then, later, creeping round the edge of Ewebank Farm? Did he know she had watched him pick something up in the garden at Mary Davis's house?

'Listen, Josh, when you said running out in front of a car was something you'd been planning for a long time—'

'Mr Quayle came back to see me,' he said, 'but they'd given me an injection or something so I didn't have a chance to apologise properly. I just remember him saying how the two of you had gone back to town in a taxi, and how your father—'

'When was that?' Karen interrupted. 'I mean, when did he come to see you?' She had been hoping she might bump into Peter Quayle. Now it looked as if she was too late.

'I expect he just wanted to check I was all right and there wouldn't be a court case or anything. I told him it wasn't his fault.' He looked away, pulling at the blankets with his good hand. 'Why didn't you tell the police?'

'When?' But before she could ask him to explain a door squeaked and two people entered the ward.

At the sight of them Josh lay back on his pillows and closed his eyes again. 'My parents,' he whispered. 'Look, please don't say anything. I'll be out of here by the end of the week. I'll explain everything, I promise.'

Karen stood up as Mrs Bowen approached. Josh's father had stopped to retie his shoelace. In contrast to his wife he was very tall and very dark, with receding hair that had been brushed forward to form a wispy kind of fringe. Mrs Bowen looked tired, and not very well, but Inspector Bowen seemed to be tense, keyed up. His eyes moved in all directions as if he was still on duty and it was his job to check the ward, but perhaps he was simply looking for spare chairs.

Since Josh obviously had no intention of introducing her she decided she had better do it herself. 'Karen Cady. I'm a friend of Josh's from school.'

'Karen.' Mrs Bowen gave her a warm smile. 'You were there at the time of the accident. Thank you so much for everything you did.' She turned to her husband. 'Mike, this is Karen.'

Inspector Bowen nodded, but his eyes

remained fixed on the far end of the ward. In an effort to make up for his rudeness Mrs Bowen started talking fast, telling Karen how she had heard all about what happened, how if it hadn't been for Karen no-one would have known who Josh was. She seemed to think he had been unconscious, or incapable of giving the paramedics his name, but perhaps she just wanted to express her gratitude to Karen.

Mike Bowen found another chair. He gestured to his wife to sit down and Karen took it as a way of telling her she ought to leave.

'Anyway, I hope you'll be feeling better soon,' she told Josh.

'Thanks.' His eyes met hers for a brief moment.

'After you're home I'll give you a ring, just to see how you are.'

Josh said nothing so Mrs Bowen filled what would have been an awkward silence with yet more thanks for everything Karen had done. 'And do call round at the house. You'd be more than welcome, wouldn't she, Mike?'

As she walked down the hospital corridor she

wondered why Josh's father had been so unfriendly, almost hostile, towards her. Perhaps he was like that to everyone. Anyway, there were far more important things to think about than Inspector Bowen. Why Josh had run in front of Peter Quayle's car on purpose? Why he had asked her if she had been to the police, then begged her to do nothing until he came out of hospital and had an opportunity to explain?

# Seven

Since Tessie knew nothing about Josh Bowen it was difficult for Karen to explain why she had accompanied him in the ambulance, then visited him in hospital.

'I was the only person at the scene of the accident who knew who he was.'

'Lucky you were there,' said Tessie suspiciously.

'Yes.' They were sitting on Tessie's bed and things felt almost like they used to be, before she had become so involved with the petition. Karen had been dying to tell her about Peter Quayle, how they'd sat together in the back of a taxi, then how he had insisted on buying her a coffee. 'It was Peter Quayle's car,' she said, 'only it wasn't his fault, Josh just ran out into the road.'

'Peter Quayle? You mean the man who lives in Stockwood House? I saw him on the telly not long ago. He's awful, really conceited.'

'No, he's not at all like that,' said Karen. 'Anyway, I'd be quite pleased with myself if I'd started all those businesses.'

Tessie screwed up her nose. 'You'd have to be really hard to be that successful. Anyway, I just think about poor Esme. She used to lie awake at night, wondering which room he slept in and whether the old bath and basin had been replaced by a new ivory suite with gold taps.'

Karen laughed, but Tessie obviously didn't think it was funny.

'She really disliked him. I think she felt he'd stolen her old home.'

'But that's ridiculous,' said Karen. 'Anyway, she and Peter never actually met.'

Tessie stared at her. 'Yes, they did. At the County Show. Esme always went to it, to make sure the animals were being properly looked after. When she was there last year Peter Quayle came up to her and introduced himself.'

'You're sure about that?'

'Yes, of course I'm sure. I remember her saying how he'd gone on and on about the house and how wonderful it was. It really upset her.'

'I expect he was trying to be kind. I expect he wanted her to know how much he appreciated it.' But Karen was wondering why Peter had lied to her. Perhaps she had misunderstood, he had just meant he didn't know Esme Fitch well. Perhaps he had forgotten about the County Show.

'Esme thought he was deliberately rubbing it in,' said Tessie.

'That's silly, he was only being friendly. Anyway, I like him.'

'Bit old for you, isn't he?'

'Oh, for heaven's sake. Anyway, what about you and Billy Henderson, he looks at least twenty-two.'

'He's twenty,' said Tessie, 'and I told you before, he's just someone who shares the same interests, thinks there's more to life than buying lots of clothes and CDs.'

Karen decided not to mention the fact that

Tessie had at least three times as many clothes as she did. Instead, she asked where Billy lived.

'In a room in a house in Southfield Road. His parents own a big house in one of those villages a few miles off the motorway, but Billy doesn't really get on with them. He thinks that in about ten years time everything will have changed. There won't be many jobs so people will only work part-time. Their standard of living will be much lower, only they'll be happier because they'll have different values, better ones.'

Karen decided to change the subject. 'You know Craig and Selina?'

'What about them?'

'Billy doesn't seem to think much of them. He said Selina was a bit of a nutcase.'

'When did he say that?'

'I told you, I was helping to clear the footpath, we walked back to the shops.'

Tessie glared at her. 'Selina's mother ran off when she was still a baby and she was brought up in a children's home until she was ten. Then they made her go and live with her grandmother.'

'*Made* her?'

'The grandmother was horrible, and really old. She didn't want Selina, just thought she'd be useful round the house.'

Karen smiled. 'You make her sound like Cinderella.'

'Yes, well you've obviously made up your mind about her just because she's got a nose-ring and doesn't like wearing shoes. Anyway, next time you see Billy you can tell him I've got the leaflets about factory farming – if he still wants them.'

'I won't be seeing him again,' said Karen. 'I can't stand another afternoon clearing that path.'

Stockwood House was on a hill above the village. The road going up to it was so steep that even someone on a mountain bike would have had difficulty keeping the pedals turning. Karen's bike was not in that class. She hid it behind a hedge and started up the hill on foot. The air was heavy and flying insects buzzed round her head. She broke off a branch of bracken to use as a swat, but it didn't do much good so she dropped it in a ditch that was full of stagnant water. Whenever she thought she had reached the top there was another bend in the road and still no view of the house. Eventually she thought she could see tall iron gates in the distance and, when she grew closer, all she could see was a winding driveway with a mass of purple rhododendrons on either side, and thick woods behind them.

If she started down the drive she might meet someone, even Peter Quayle in his four-wheel-drive off-roader. It would be better to stay on the road and hope it would soon be possible to see the house through a gap in the hedge. The rhododendrons were past their best and the whole place had a slightly gloomy feel, but on a bright summer's day it probably looked pretty good.

In the effort of climbing the hill she had almost forgotten why she had come. Even now she wasn't sure. Because Peter Quayle had deliberately misled her when he told her he and Esme Fitch had never met? But what good would it do, gawping at Stockwood House? Was it possible Esme had been threatening him in some way? Perhaps she had known something about his early career, something that would have ruined his image, or even put him in prison. Perhaps she had had papers hidden in the bungalow, and had been planning to use them as incriminating evidence.

Now that she was high up the wind was stronger, but the climb had made her hot and sticky and she was glad of the cool air. She paused to take a rather dusty mint from her pocket, then rounded yet another corner and there it was. The hedge was only about a metre high and the first thing that caught her eye was a large lake. The water was moving, blown by the wind into tiny ripples, and beyond it, on a flat ridge, was the house.

She had no idea how old it was. If Esme's family had lived there for several generations she supposed that meant it must have been built at least two hundred years ago. The house itself was not particularly attractive, and the gardens had been laid out in a kind of formal pattern. Wide paths surrounded perfect stretches of grass, and neat box hedges surrounded the outside edges of the paths. Stone steps led up to a summerhouse that looked as if it had views in all directions.

As she gazed down at the scene it occurred to her that it could have been Esme Fitch, not Peter Quayle, who had lied. Still bitter, even after all those years, at having to give up Stockwood, she had invented a meeting with Peter and given everyone the impression he had gloated over her and made her feel even worse.

There was no sign of the Shogun, but it could be in the garage which probably had space for four or five cars. A gardener was crouched over one of the flowerbeds. He straightened up, brushing back his bushy grey hair with the back of his hand, and Karen realised it was a woman dressed in heavy cord trousers. She called to someone, shading her eyes with her hand, and an Old English sheepdog appeared, wagging its stumpy tail, then rolling on its back on the grass.

Peter Quayle probably had a staff of gardeners, cleaners, and cooks. Karen wondered why he had never married, then remembered he was still in his early thirties. The woman who had stepped out of his car, just before Josh's accident, must be his girlfriend. She tried to remember if she had seen her before, but she had looked like so many rich, smart people, with her expensive clothes and immaculately groomed hair.

After watching the gardener for a short time she decided to return to the village. The compulsion to see the house had been simply to satisfy her curiosity. In the village, if she was lucky, she might find someone who had known Esme Fitch before the Fitch family had to sell up and move out. She might even meet someone who knew Peter Quayle.

There was nothing picturesque about the village. It sprawled along the main road, the houses becoming older and smaller as she moved closer to the centre, which turned out to be just a patch of grass and a boarded-up shop. There was hardly anyone about, just a man sitting on a bench reading a newspaper, and a woman who was strapping a baby into a car seat. A path led to the church. Karen walked under the low wooden archway, hoping the building was left open during the day, and glancing at the gravestones as she passed. There were no Fitches, but if any of the family had been buried there they probably had a special plot.

The church door was closed, but when she gave the heavy iron ring a twist it came open with a creak, and she stepped inside, breathing in the musty smell that all churches seemed to have in common. At first she thought it was empty, then a very small man in a long black cassock appeared, carrying a pile of hymn-books. He approached her and she expected him to say something, but he just nodded and carried on walking to a ledge just inside the main entrance where he started stacking up the hymn-books.

Karen waited a moment, pretending to be interested in a stained-glass window, then she moved closer to the man, trying to think of a way of engaging him in conversation.

He was the first to speak. 'Just moved into The Gables, have you? I heard it was a large family; the village could do with more young people.'

'No. No, I don't live here. I came on my bike.'

'You're interested in churches?' The man was still stacking hymn-books so she couldn't see his face, but his voice sounded as if he thought she was up to no good.

'I came down the hill from Stockwood House,' she said. 'I mean, I saw the house from the top of the hill. I'd never noticed it before and I didn't realise there was a lake.'

He finished stacking the hymn-books and started picking up the petals that had dropped from a vase of yellow flowers. Now that she could see him properly she was surprised to discover how old he looked. About eighty, she guessed, or even older. Did vicars stay on in their parishes until they dropped?

'So you heard about Miss Fitch,' he said, suddenly sitting down heavily at one end of a wooden pew.

Karen opened her mouth to deny that her visit had anything to do with Esme Fitch, then changed her mind. 'Yes, wasn't it terrible? I knew her a bit. She was interested in helping to protect the environment. Are you the vicar?'

The old man smiled. 'Used to be, for over forty years. Now I just give the new one a hand. After I retired they joined three parishes together; St

Stephen's, St Andrew's, and St Mary the Virgin.'

'So you must have known Miss Fitch when she was still living in Stockwood House.'

He found a large white handkerchief and sneezed several times. Karen couldn't help noticing that his cassock was rather shabby and had several stains down the front. He looked a bit eccentric, but his eyes were exceptionally bright and his mind seemed perfectly clear.

'Dusty places, churches,' he said. 'You tell me Esme was a friend of yours?'

Karen nodded. 'It was an awful shock, hearing what had happened. It must have been an accident, don't you think? I mean, no-one would have done such a thing deliberately.'

The old man looked at her curiously. 'The house has been bought by Peter Quayle,' he said. 'Before that it was some people called Longley, only they were abroad for most of the year so I never understood why they wanted the place. Of course, when Quayle bought it people could see there was a kind of rough justice.'

'Justice?' Karen tried to sound interested, but not so curious that he would become suspicious.

'You don't know what happened then?' he said slowly. 'Of course you don't. Must be getting on for thirty years ago. Anyway, that's all in the past. Now, would you let me show you a rather amusing little window?'

'Oh.' She was disappointed. 'Yes. Thank you very much.'

He led her to the far end of the church where there was a small side chapel, then pointed to a tiny diamond-shaped window with blue edging and a picture of a tree covered in little purple berries.

'Plumtree,' announced the old man. 'He was the vicar here back at the turn of the century. Bit small for plums, I've always thought, but it's rather delightful, don't you think?'

'It's lovely.' Karen had never had a particular interest in stained-glass windows, but she couldn't help picking up some of the old man's enthusiasm.

He took her by the arm and just as she thought he was going to lead her out of the church, and maybe lock it up, he stopped and gave her a cheerful smile. 'Before you go, you'll want me to tell you about Peter Quayle's father. You've heard rumours, I expect, but the story became distorted, embroidered.'

Karen knew nothing about Peter's father or any connection with Esme, but she was intrigued so wasn't about to stop him in full flow.

'Yes, I had heard something.' It was a lie, but what else could she say?

They sat side by side on a long polished bench. 'Quayle must have been a baby,' he said, 'certainly not more than two or three. His father was the chauffeur, used to drive Esme's parents up to London now and again, or sometimes he'd just take them out for a spin. Esme must have been in her late thirties. Her younger brother had married and moved to the Yorkshire Dales, but she told you that I expect.'

'Actually, she never said much about him.'

'No, well, I don't suppose she would. I believe they lost touch after the tragedy.' He paused, studying the veins on the back of his hands. 'No-one ever knew why Quayle lost his job. Patrick Quayle, that is. There were rumours, of course, all kinds of speculations, but you know what village people are. Be that as it may, the following day he took the car out on his own and crashed it head on into a high stone wall.'

'He was killed? You mean he did it on purpose?'

The old man looked deep into her eyes. 'I prefer to think he was not quite of sound mind, too distraught to know what he was doing. Of course, within a month Marianne had disappeared.'

'Marianne was Peter Quayle's mother?'

He nodded slowly. 'Beautiful girl. Long red hair, not unlike your own. That's why all the stories were so hard to believe.' He stood up slowly, and waited for her to do the same. 'Now, come along, my dear, you say you don't live in the village so I expect it's time you were getting on home.'

# *Eight*

Peter Quayle was opening the new out-of-town hypermarket. Karen asked Tessie and Billy if they would like to go with her, but neither seemed all that keen.

'I don't know how you can,' said Tessie, 'after everything Esme did to try and stop it being built.'

'Yes, well I thought you'd be demonstrating or something. You could always carry a banner.'

'Bit late for that,' said Billy. 'All the same, I'd have gone with you, just for a laugh, only I promised I'd do some collecting, door to door. What's he like, that Quayle bloke? Tessie said you'd had a ride in his car.'

'No, only in a taxi. A boy was knocked down and we had to go to the hospital.'

Tessie was arranging piles of leaflets on the trestle-table. From the expression on her face she thought Karen should either help or go away. Billy smiled at Karen, then nodded in Tessie's direction and pulled a face. Karen nodded. So she wasn't the only one who believed Tessie was beginning to take herself far too seriously.

It was starting to drizzle and the walk to the outskirts of the town wasn't going to be much fun, but if she took a bus she would be there too soon. She had to talk to Peter and, short of calling in at Stockwood House, it could be her only chance.

On her way up Larkhill Road she saw Mrs Bowen. She had parked her car near the old swimming-baths, where there was a one hour limit but the parking was free. When she climbed out of her car she looked as if she was in a tearing hurry but as soon as she saw Karen she tried to give the impression she had all the time in the world.

'Karen, how nice to see you. Where are you off to, or do you live near here?'

Karen asked after Josh.

'Oh, he's much better. They were a little worried about the arm, afraid it might have to be reset, but now the doctor thinks it's going to be all right after all.'

'But they're still keeping him in for a few more days?'

Mrs Bowen looked a little flustered. 'Only two or three, just to be on the safe side.'

'Yes, I see.' Karen was wondering if Josh really wanted to leave. Hospital was safe, a refuge. When he returned home she would be one of his first visitors, and he would have to answer a string of questions. 'I'm going to see Peter Quayle opening the new hypermarket,' she said, 'not that I'm all that interested in hypermarkets but I thought, in the circumstances . . .'

'Yes, of course. If you speak to him do give him my best wishes. He came to see us, you know. I thought he was charming.'

Mrs Bowen looked exhausted. She could have been really pretty but she didn't seem to care how she looked. Karen felt sorry for her, but she wasn't sure why. Obviously she must be worried about Josh, but her dowdy appearance couldn't have come about overnight. Her hair was flat and lifeless – not that hair was ever alive, apart from in television commercials – and her clothes looked as if they had lain in a crumpled heap, then been put on again because she couldn't be bothered to find any others.

'Josh's father,' said Mrs Bowen, still smiling too much, still trying to sound as if she hadn't a worry in the world, 'he has a slightly off-putting manner but he doesn't mean to be rude. In the hospital . . . I thought perhaps . . .'

'I expect he was worried about Josh,' said Karen, 'and it must be difficult for him, fitting in visits, now he's working on the two break-ins and one of them might turn out to be murder.'

Mrs Bowen steadied herself, holding on to the iron railings that ran between the pavement and the ring road on the other side. 'How did you know that? Did Josh tell you?'

'No, I don't think it was Josh. I forget.'

Just before she walked away Mrs Bowen cleared her throat and pretended she had just thought of something, only it was not really very important. 'Oh, Karen, Josh hasn't said anything, has he?'

'What about?'

She chewed her lip, wondering whether to say more. 'No, it's all right, I didn't think he would have. It's just, he's so few friends, well, none that I know of, but of course it takes time to settle into a new school, doesn't it?'

Karen had expected a large crowd, but when she thought about it Peter Quayle hardly had the same drawing power as a pop singer or an actor from a soap opera. Those who *had* turned up were probably there for the vouchers for free goods which the first hundred customers were due to receive. Karen joined them on the imitation cobbled walkway and watched the staff, in their brand new uniforms, assemble outside the main entrance. The drizzle had stopped, but the sky was still overcast and the atmosphere unpleasantly humid.

It was a long, boring wait. She knew Peter Quayle was there – she could see the Shogun parked round the side of the building – but although the opening had been scheduled for eleven o'clock, it was nearly a quarter past before the manager emerged, accompanied by Peter, who was dressed in jeans, a pale blue sweatshirt, and desert boots.

Even though she liked him she couldn't help feeling there was something just a little phoney about his appearance. How could jeans and a sweatshirt look so expensive? But they did. He was smiling at the crowd, running his fingers through his hair, shaking hands with someone from the bakery who was dressed in a gleaming white overall and tall white hat.

The manager made a short speech, then Peter Quayle made another. After that he was handed a large pair of scissors, and with the cameras flashing all round, cut through a ridiculous white ribbon, before standing back to allow the first shoppers through the automatic doors.

Karen was curious to see how such an enormous building could be filled. Presumably they were going to sell clothes as well as food and household stuff. There was probably a restaurant too, and an optician's and somewhere to get your films developed. Another time maybe. Just now she had to keep her eyes firmly fixed on the Shogun and try to catch Peter before he drove away.

About twenty minutes later he emerged from a side door. It was no good approaching him directly, not with the store manager and his deputy thanking him profusely, then standing about, waiting to see him off. Karen walked quickly towards the exit and positioned herself where it would be difficult for him to miss her. The Shogun was moving slowly across the carpark. Waving her arms would look stupid, stepping out in front of him would seem like a repeat of Josh's reckless behaviour. Instead, she kept her eyes glued on him, willing him to notice who she was.

'Karen?' He slowed to a stop, then lowered his electrically operated window. 'Didn't expect to see you here. Not exactly your scene, is it?'

'I wanted to ask you something.'

'So you came all the way out here? You should've given me a ring.'

'I thought you'd be ex-directory. You must be, surely.'

He laughed. 'Hop in, then, I'll give you a lift back to town and you can ask me on the way. Sounds intriguing.' Then his voice became serious. 'Or is it about Josh?'

'No, nothing like that.'

Now he was smiling to himself, probably imagining he was so amazingly attractive she couldn't keep away. Well, in that case, he was in for a shock. He started talking about the hypermarket and how it had the largest fruit and vegetable section in the country, then he launched into a description of how the deputy manager had shown him a display of exotic-looking fish with bulging eyes and silvery scales. Karen listened attentively, but when they reached the roundabout that led to the motorway, or back to the city, she decided it was time to interrupt.

'Esme Fitch,' she said, sounding more stern than she had meant to. 'You said you'd never met her, but what about the time you introduced yourself to her at the County Show?'

He hesitated, but only for a second. 'Yes,

you're absolutely right. She was so irate I suppose I blocked the incident out of my mind. I felt sorry for her, I really did, but she could hardly hold me responsible for the fact that her parents had to sell Stockwood.'

Karen had expected him to deny the meeting ever took place. His response had thrown her a little, but she ploughed on, determined to find out as much as she could. 'You must have been pleased when it came on the market.'

His head came round fast. 'Why d'you say that?'

'Oh, no reason, only I was talking to an old man in the village . . .' Already she was regretting her remark, but it was too late, there was no going back.

'Which old man was that?' said Peter. 'No, don't tell me, it could've been any one of a dozen or more. Like all villages it's alive with gossip, some of it about things that happened donkey's years ago, and most of it, I suspect, entirely without basis. Incidentally, what were you doing in the village?'

'I went there on my bike.'

'You went there on your bike,' he repeated. 'And?'

'I met the vicar, I mean, the ex-vicar, and he showed me a stained-glass window.'

'And the conversation gradually came round to the fascinating subject of Patrick Quayle.'

'Look, it's nothing to do with me, but—'

'Too right. And since it all happened over thirty years ago I don't see how you could possibly have any interest, apart from some morbid curiosity fuelled no doubt by Esme Fitch's violent death. No, don't say any more. Anyway, what business is it of yours? You enjoy playing amateur detective, do you? Now, shall we change the subject? You've seen Josh, I expect. I hear they were a little worried about his arm but the problem's been sorted out and he'll be home in a couple of days.'

Karen stared through the car window, seeing the stream of traffic travelling in the opposite direction but taking in nothing. She had ruined her friendship with Peter Quayle, just because she had got into her head that it might be just remotely possible he had some connection with the break-in at Esme Fitch's bungalow. *Her friendship with Peter Quayle?* Who was she fooling? As far as he was concerned she was just some kid who had seen Josh Bowen run out into the road and would confirm to the police that the accident hadn't been his fault.

The Shogun had that brand-new smell her father always insisted was sprayed on to the seats with an aerosol. She racked her brains for something to say, something that would put them back on friendly terms. In the end, all she could come up with was a stupid remark about how much she liked the car.

He shrugged. 'It serves its purpose.'

'I expect you've got others too. Alex, my stepfather, has got an old Volkswagen he's stripping down.' She despised herself for being so hypocritical. 'So I'm quite interested in cars.'

Peter smiled, aware that she was trying to make amends for prying into his private life. 'I used to have a Ferrari,' he said, 'but it disappeared off the face of the earth. Probably stolen to order, then resprayed, given new number plates, and shipped to the Middle East.'

After Peter had dropped her off she walked slowly back to the flat, cursing herself all the way for making such a mess of everything. Nothing had been achieved. Instead of gradually leading up to the subject, she had told him straight out how she had cycled to the village, and hadn't even bothered to invent a plausible cover story. No wonder he had reacted badly.

She could see the outline of her father's head. He was seated at the computer and she could just make out the flicker of the screen. If he was in a good mood she might tell him about the opening of the hypermarket. She might even tell him about Peter Quayle's father and the mystery surrounding the way he had been sacked, then crashed the Fitches' family car into a wall.

'Got a minute?' The voice behind her was so close that Karen let out an involuntary gasp.

When she turned round Selina was standing there, leaning against the wall. She had changed the colour of her hair and dispensed with the beads, but there was no mistaking the skimpy skirt, skin-tight tee-shirt and torn tights. 'Your dad's a detective, right?'

'What about it?'

'No, it doesn't matter.' She moved as if to walk away, then changed her mind and faced Karen again.

'What doesn't matter?' said Karen.

Selina twisted one of the row of gold studs in her left ear. 'Thing is, you want to know what happened to that Fitch woman, right? Only it's not how it looks.'

'What isn't how it looks?'

'People,' said Selina, 'like the one you was talking to earlier. People aren't always what they look. I'd be careful if I was you, and don't say nothing about me telling you, 'cos that'd just make it worse, know what I mean?'

'No, all right, but I don't understand. The person I was talking to earlier? You mean Peter Quayle?'

'Old people,' she said. 'Get all bitter, don't they?'

'Yes, I suppose so, some of them. It depends who they are.'

Selina's face was frighteningly expressionless. 'Some people reckon if they're funny in the head they'd be better off dead.'

Karen shuddered slightly. 'Are you talking about Esme Fitch? She wasn't even seventy.'

She shrugged, then started walking away, calling over her shoulder just before she turned the corner, 'Anyway, I've told you. Up to you now, ain't it?'

# Nine

In two days time her mother and Alex would be back. Karen had received six postcards, one every other day, all written by her mother apart from Alex's abbey, although on some of the other cards he had done silly drawings of wine bottles and frogs' legs.

'You're sure I couldn't stay on here?' she asked her father.

'Don't be ridiculous.'

They both knew it had been only a token request. Helping her father in the office worked really well, but living with him in such a small space was a different matter.

'I met Peter Quayle again,' she said.

'Oh, yes.' Her father was sorting through a pile

of papers. 'How did that come about?'

She was going to say Quayle had given her a lift in the Shogun, then she thought better of it. 'Oh, he was just doing some shopping.'

'Down here most of the time now, or so I've heard. I suppose it's possible to run your businesses from home these days. I expect he has a whole room at Stockwood House entirely devoted to computers and fax machines.'

'He opened the new hypermarket,' she said, wanting to tell him what she had found out about Peter Quayle's father. 'By the way, are the police making any progress with the Esme Fitch case?'

'I couldn't say, Karen.' He still hadn't found what he was looking for and he sounded as if he was working himself up into one of his moods.

'What about Mary Davis, is she out of hospital yet? I expect she'll have to go and stay with one of her children, to convalesce. D'you know where they live?'

'What? Look, if you've nothing better to do, shouldn't you buy whatever your mother needs for when she gets back?'

'I was going to do it tomorrow.'

He turned round irritably. 'You've checked the house, watered the plants?'

She nodded. He was trying to get rid of her again. In that case he could miss out on the intriguing information about Peter Quayle's past. Maybe it was common knowledge. The retired vicar certainly wasn't the only one who knew about it. And the police?

She folded up her bedclothes and piled them up on the floor beside the sofa, then left without telling her father when she would be back. Considering she was only going to be there for two more days you would have thought he could have been a bit more pleasant. Perhaps it was nothing to do with her; he was having trouble with a client, or with the girlfriend she had never met. If she let herself think about it she felt a little upset that their two weeks together hadn't worked out as well as she had planned, but it was probably because she had expected too much. All the same, when her mother and Alex asked how everything had gone she would say 'Great, fantastic' and pretend she wished the arrangement could have continued indefinitely.

It was one of those days when everyone you see reminds you of somebody else. A man running down the steps from the library looked just like Alex but turned out to be at least ten years younger. A woman carrying four bulging plastic bags reminded her of Josh's mother but, on closer inspection, even Mrs Bowen didn't look as harassed as that.

She had been thinking about Peter Quayle. Perhaps he had got his revenge. Well, that was the way she saw it. The son of a chauffeur, who had started his own business and made enough to buy the house that had once belonged to the people responsible for his father's death. People talked about deprived childhoods, the bad effect of being brought up by only one parent and without much money, but was it really that simple? The determination to overcome difficulties could spur you on. The wish for revenge was surely the strongest motive of all.

She was walking in a part of the city she had never visited before. Just walking and thinking, partly about her father, but mainly she was trying to sort out everything she knew about Esme Fitch, all the pieces of seemingly useless information that wouldn't fit together into anything that made any sense.

Lost in thought, it was pure chance that she happened to look up and see the driver of a passing car. When the lights changed the car had to slow down and then there was no doubt who it was. But how could it be? Just for a moment the colour of the hair convinced her she had made a mistake. Then she realised that, under the blue and white baseball cap, the driver must be wearing a wig. But why would somebody with a perfectly good head of hair choose to wear a rather unflattering wig? And the car, it was brand new, a black BMW.

Watching it disappear round the corner, she felt a flutter of apprehension in her stomach. Apprehension, or perhaps, since she had left the flat without having anything to eat, it was really just hunger. Making a mental note of the time and the place, she crossed the road, took what she hoped was a short cut, and set off in the direction of the motorway service station where she would be able to buy a Coke and some chips.

The self-service restaurant was packed. Karen bought her chips at the burger bar, ate them standing up, then wandered into the shop. She liked service stations. Even though this particular one was on the edge of the city, rather than miles out in the country, you still picked up the feeling that everyone was on the way to somewhere else, and you could do what you liked because you were highly unlikely to see any of the people ever again. Everything in the shop was grossly overpriced. She flicked through one or two magazines, then started inspecting the cuddly toys. Something that looked like a pink gorilla cost £16.50. The teddy bear was slightly cheaper but had a squint in one of its yellow plastic eyes.

'Karen?' Hearing her name she jumped violently, then spun round and came face to face with Josh's mother.

'Oh, hello.' She could see at once that Mrs Bowen had been crying. The small amount of make-up she was wearing looked streaky and there were black smudges of mascara below her eyes.

The two of them looked at each other for a moment, then Karen started explaining how she had been for a long walk, then realised how hungry she was and called in at the service station for some chips.

Mrs Bowen listened politely. 'I thought perhaps you were with your parents, buying petrol or something. My car's in the carpark. I just dropped in to buy some sweets. They're for Josh's brother.'

'Oh.' For the first time it occurred to her that since it was the holidays her other son must be at home. 'He goes to boarding school, doesn't he? Well, that's what a boy in Josh's class told me.'

She drew in breath sharply. 'Josh has told people about his brother?'

'Mark Hill. I don't know if you've met him. Or I suppose someone else might have told Mark. Where is the school?'

Mrs Bowen was still breathing hard. 'You're in a hurry, I expect, only I wondered if I couldn't possibly buy you a cup of coffee?'

'Yes. I mean, thanks.' Karen had no idea what had prompted the offer but it seemed rude to refuse.

They left the shop and Mrs Bowen pushed open the door to the restaurant. 'You could have something to eat if you like.' Then, when Karen shook her head, 'No, I'm not hungry either.'

'We don't have to wait in the queue,' said Karen, 'not if we're only buying drinks.'

'No, of course not, how stupid.' Mrs Bowen had a slightly wild-eyed look. She hurried towards the drinks counter, ordered two coffees, found money for the cashier, and scanned the seating area, searching for a table as far away from everyone else as possible.

When they sat down she swallowed several times, then started talking very fast. 'I'm telling you this, Karen, because I don't know what else to do. I suppose I could talk to Josh's year tutor, but what good would it do? I know he's not in your class but at least . . .' She hesitated, rubbing the corner of her eye as if there was something in it. 'He seems to like you.'

'Is that what he said?' It seemed rather unlikely.

A man in a shiny suit was taking food off a tray: fried fish with peas, double chips, a plate of bread and butter, pot of tea, several sachets of tomato sauce and mayonnaise, a jam doughnut and a Danish pastry.

'The way he was telling me about how you went with him in the ambulance,' said Mrs Bowen.

'It was the first time we'd met properly.' How could she explain that although she knew next to nothing about him there was a kind of invisible bond between her and Josh, because of the way she had watched him shop-lifting, then, several days later, seen him in Mary Davis's garden, picking something up and putting it in his pocket? 'Anyway, if there's anything I can do to help . . .'

'Have you lived in this area long? I expect you've lots of friends. Brothers and sisters?'

'No.' She decided she had better say something about herself. 'I'm an only child. My parents are divorced. I live with my mother and her new husband, but just at the moment they're on holiday so I'm staying with my father.'

'Yes, I see. What children have to put up with these days. When I was young it was all so different, but not really, I suppose. Things went on behind closed doors instead of—' She broke off. 'Your father lives locally then?'

'Yes, he's a private detective. He used to be in the police, then he left to set up his own business. I work in his office during the school holidays, if he needs anything put into the computer, or to answer the phone if . . .'

Mrs Bowen had stopped listening. 'Stevie,' she said dreamily. 'He's thirteen, but big for his age, taller than Josh.'

'Stevie is Josh's brother?'

She nodded. Her coffee was untouched. She kept stirring it, automatically, as if she was not aware of what she was doing. 'He lived with us until he was nine, then it got too much for me. I just couldn't cope. Of course, even when he was quite a small baby I realised there was something wrong. Josh is so kind, so patient, but my husband's never been able to accept what happened. I think he hoped Stevie would grow out of it, or someone would find some miracle cure.'

Karen wanted to ask what was wrong with Stevie but it seemed wrong to interrupt.

'The doctors have never agreed on a diagnosis,' said Mrs Bowen. 'For a time Mike was convinced we should go to America so Stevie could take park in a special programme, but we couldn't possibly have afforded it even if we'd remortgaged the house, and I know in his heart of hearts he knew it was a waste of time.'

'I'm sorry.' Karen struggled to find the right words, but whatever she said, what difference would it make?

'When things got really difficult Mike asked for a transfer.'

'Yes, I see.' Karen waited for an explanation, but it was some time coming.

'Friends,' said Mrs Bowen at last, 'and the Social Services. Mike thought people were trying to put pressure on him. He thought we should have a new start.' She took a sip of her coffee. 'I was hoping Josh had told you about it. He's so terribly, terribly angry.'

'About Stevie?'

'Oh no, he was still so young when Stevie was

born he just accepts him the way he is. Until today he's always come with me to see his brother. As I said Stevie's a big boy, and he gets so excited when we take him out I could never manage on my own, not now, not when I have to drive the car. I tried it once but he started pulling at me, kissing me, and we nearly had an accident. After that I decided it needed the two of us unless I just visited him at the home, but then he'd have been so disappointed.'

'What about your husband?'

'Mike? Oh, I thought you understood. He prefers to pretend Stevie doesn't exist. "What difference does it make?" That's what he keeps saying. "He doesn't even know who we are." But it's not true, I know it's not. Josh's accident, you don't think . . . Lately he's been so quiet, he won't tell me anything, and he won't even speak to his father. I think he really hates him.'

Karen was shocked, but not because Josh hated his father. She would have felt the same in his situation. 'If there's anything I can do . . .' She wanted to say what she thought of Mike Bowen, but in her experience people could tell you dreadful things about members of their own family, and then, if you agreed, they usually sprang to the person's defence.

'I wondered,' said Mrs Bowen, 'I know it's a lot to ask, but if you would speak to Josh, maybe you could persuade him to tell you how he's feeling. The way he's going he'll make himself ill, or do something . . .' She couldn't bring herself to finish the sentence.

'I'll try,' said Karen, 'but I'm not sure if it'll do any good.'

Mrs Bowen managed a smile. 'Thank you so much. He'll be coming out of hospital the day after tomorrow. Perhaps if you came round to the house.' She searched her bag for a pen and something to write the address on. 'Not in the evening, of course, although Mike probably wouldn't be there. He's out till all hours at the moment.' She stood up. 'I must go now. Stevie's got no sense of time, but the staff will have told him I'm coming and he'll be waiting at the window. I won't take him out, of course, but the sweets will make him happy, and this.' She held up a brown paper bag. 'A car transporter. Stevie's mad on car transporters. Goodbye for now and if you think you can come round I'd be ever so grateful.'

# Ten

It was nearly two o'clock. After she had waved goodbye to Mrs Bowen, Karen decided to walk as far as the Park and Ride carpark, then catch the bus back to the city centre. Tuesday was one of the days for collecting more signatures for the petition, but if she hung around till three-thirty Tessie and her fellow workers usually started to pack up at about that time.

Karen wanted to talk to Tessie, not about what Mrs Bowen had just told her – that would be breaking a confidence – but she needed to find out if there was any way Josh could have known Esme Fitch. She remembered Tessie's mother mentioning how some of Josh's year at school had taken part in a scheme Esme had organised shortly before she died. The aim was to decorate people's houses when they were too old or infirm to do it themselves, but things had gone wrong when two idiots sloshed white paint over an old man's living-room carpet. It seemed unlikely Josh would have taken part in the scheme, but there was just a chance.

The bus was almost empty, but it started to fill up as they approached the city centre. Karen sat at the back, hoping no-one would join her. She was thinking about Mike Bowen and wondering how someone could reject their own son. Did it happen quite often, a parent so upset about their brain-damaged child that they pretended he, or she, had never been born? She tried to see it from Inspector Bowen's point of view, but it was hard. Then she thought about Josh. Was he so angry with his father that the shop-lifting had been an attempt to get himself arrested, end up at the police station, then get a grim satisfaction from telling them his name and whose son he was? When that failed it was possible he had decided to do something more serious. Break into Mary Davis's house? He could have forced a window, come face to face with the old lady, then, in the struggle to get away, accidentally pushed her to the ground. Whatever he had picked up from the garden could be something he knew he had dropped. But wouldn't the police have found it? Then there was Esme Fitch. She was certain Josh would never have gone that far, but if he was desperate enough he might be prepared to let people think he had been involved in some way.

The bus pulled up outside C & A and Karen jumped off, glanced at her watch, and nearly fell over a large pair of feet.

'Sorry.' She looked up and realised the feet belonged to Billy's friend, Craig. 'It's Craig, isn't it? I'm a friend of Tessie's – and Billy's.'

'And your father's a private eye, right? What does he do? Go round in an old mac, spying on people cheating on their wives?'

Karen sighed. 'Have you seen Tessie?'

'Starting to pack up now. I guess everyone who's likely to sign the petition has been and gone.'

'Yes, I expect so.' In spite of his silly remarks he seemed quite friendly. He was grossly overweight, but that wasn't a crime, even if you were only nineteen or twenty.

'Had a mate once who consulted a private detective,' he said. 'Your father been brought in yet, to help find who beat up the old dears?'

'No, that's up to the police.'

'S'pose it would be.' He fingered his upper lip. 'Billy was fond of that one that got done in. He thinks the cops should've got whoever done it by now. I reckon if he had the money he'd ask your dad to make a few inquiries. As for the second one who had her house done over, she may not have snuffed it but I reckon, seeing she was an invalid, that was nearly as bad.'

'Mrs Davis was an invalid?' That was news to Karen. 'Who told you that?'

'Friend of my mum's,' said Craig. 'She couldn't leave the house, had to have a nurse in twice a day.'

'So it was the nurse who found her?'

He shrugged. 'Who knows? Could've been a neighbour, anyone.'

Selina was coming down the street. She had changed the colour of her hair and she was wearing a black dress with a plunging neckline. She ignored Karen and started whispering to Craig, who screwed up his face in an effort to hear what she was saying. She wasn't going to mention the time she had tried to warn Karen about people not always being how they looked. She was going to pretend the conversation had never happened.

As Karen walked away something was bothering her. Something that didn't tie up. It couldn't be anything Craig had said so perhaps she was still thinking about Josh.

Billy's hand was resting on Tessie's shoulder. Their heads were close together and Billy was talking in a low, confidential voice.

'Oh, hello, Karen.' Tessie moved away from Billy, but not without giving him a gooey-eyed smile. 'Look.' She held out the clipboard with its three pages of signatures.

'Where are you going to send it?' said Karen.

Billy laughed. 'Waste of time, you think? Well, you may be right, but somebody has to do something and pressure groups have been known to have quite an effect.'

'Yes, he's right,' said Tessie smugly. 'Look at the Green Party. Everyone used to laugh at it, now most of their ideas are being taken seriously.'

'I expect you're right.' Karen felt tired. She wanted Billy to go away so she could talk to Tessie about Josh. She would start by telling her about the shop-lifting, then go on to describe how he had walked round Ewebank Farm. If Tessie listened properly, took what she was saying seriously, she might mention the fact that he seemed to have problems at home.

'Right,' said Billy, 'I'm off. Oh, by the way, Karen, that Peter Quayle bloke you're so impressed with—'

'No, I'm not. Who said—'

'Only I was talking to this old guy who knew the Fitch family when they were still living in Stockwood House. There may not be a word of truth in it, but he said Esme'd had this thing about the family chauffeur, then when it wasn't reciprocated she'd accused him of stealing some jewellery.'

Tessie was outraged. 'Esme would never

have done a thing like that.'

'No,' said Billy, 'that's what I thought, only it was thirty years ago, or more. Anyway, the poor guy got the sack and the following day he was killed in some kind of road accident.'

'And you're telling me it was Esme's fault?' squealed Tessie. 'Just because she's dead and can't defend herself. Maybe he had stolen the jewellery, maybe the whole story's a pack of lies.'

'Calm down.' Billy's hand had returned to Tessie's shoulder. 'Only it's best to keep an open mind, wouldn't you say, Karen? Esme had probably mellowed with age. Anyway, she could be kind of reckless, you know that, Tess.'

'That's not the same as telling lies so someone lost their job.'

'No, but look at all that stuff she said about Lydia Parfrey. It's a whole person thing, alternative medicine, mind and body working together. No good just sitting there, waiting to be cured.'

Tessie was watching him curiously. 'I didn't know you were interested in homeopathy.'

'I'm not, not really. Herbalism – now that's a

different matter. I've even thought of training as a herbalist, but to do it properly it would be better to qualify as a doctor first and I'm not sure I could take seven years surrounded by idiotic medical students.'

After Billy left Karen helped Tessie and another girl fold up the trestle-table. Then a man she knew by sight arrived with a small van and started piling in the table, chairs, and display boards.

'Dougal,' said Tessie, nodding in the direction of the disappearing van. 'And the girl with him's called Frieda. She's Swedish, no, Danish, and she's really nice.'

'Yes, I'm sure.' Karen was sick of hearing about all these fantastic people. On the spur of the moment she decided to break the resolution she had made to keep the information a secret, as she was almost sure Mrs Bowen had intended her to do. 'I met Josh Bowen's mother,' she said, 'and she seemed in a pretty bad state. She told me he's got a brother who lives in a home. He's brain-damaged or something and Josh's father has disowned him. I mean he won't visit or anything so when Mrs Bowen goes to the home Josh has to go with her – to help.'

'Help? You mean the brother's in a wheelchair? How old is he?'

'No, nothing like that. He's just rather excitable and it's not safe to take him out in the car without someone there to make sure he doesn't jump all over the place.'

Tessie thought about it. 'When did Mrs Bowen tell you all this? I suppose you met her at the hospital.'

'Yes. Anyway, that's not all. Look, I can't talk here. If we walk back to your house I'll tell you on the way, only you mustn't breathe a word to anyone else. Not to Billy or Craig, and definitely not to that Selina.'

Tessie gave her a hard look. 'What's wrong with Selina?'

'You tell me. I wouldn't like to meet her in a dark alley.'

'You don't like her just because she cares about battery hens and calves being shipped abroad in container trucks.'

'Yes, well maybe you're right.' Karen didn't

want to fall out with Tessie again. 'Anyway, you and Billy seem very close. Does your mum know about it?'

'Know what? Billy's not interested in me – or you, come to that. As far as he's concerned we're just school kids, only he was warning me how I ought to be careful next time there's a demonstration. He doesn't want me getting in any trouble. Craig was arrested once and charged with assaulting a police officer.'

'He enjoys a bit of aggro? Yes, so Billy was saying, but I'd have thought Selina was more the type for that.'

None of the plants looked too bad, and the huge Swiss cheese thing that took up most of one end of the living room had even got a new pale green leaf with four symmetrical holes. Karen found a duster and ran it along the mantelpiece, then she sprayed furniture polish on the coffee table, gave it a wipe and sprayed some more in the air, just to give the place a nice clean smell. The letters, bills and junk mail were in a neat pile by the telephone. She dusted the receiver, stood staring at it as if it might bite, then picked it up and dialled Lydia Parfrey's number.

She had planned what she was going to say but when she heard Lydia's voice she nearly lost her nerve. All morning she had been practising what she hoped sounded like the voice of a frail old lady. Would Lydia be convinced, or would she realise it was a fake?

'My name's Mrs Robinson,' she said, talking much too fast. 'I was wondering if you could help me with my sinuses. You were recommended by a friend, Mary Davis.'

There was a slight pause. Karen gripped the receiver even tighter.

'I don't think I know a Mary Davis,' said Lydia, 'but I'd be happy to give you an appointment.'

'Thank you so much.' Karen struggled to maintain the deep, yet shaky voice. 'When could I come? Oh dear, I seem to have mislaid my diary. I tell you what, I'll ring back as soon as I can find it.'

After she had rung off she sat quite still for several minutes. Either Lydia Parfrey didn't want to admit that Mary Davis, as well as Esme Fitch, had been one of her clients, or there was another more alarming explanation, one that had been slowly forming in Karen's brain for the last twenty-four hours.

The bungalow in Silvester Way looked as if its owner had made an enormous effort to try and make it appear like a country cottage – with roses round the door and a great bed of lavender at the front – then given up in despair and let everything else run wild.

Karen paused by the gate, picturing the scene that must have gone on inside. Esme Fitch hearing an intruder, picking up the heaviest object she could find, opening the living-room door . . . Had it been a quick death or had she tried to crawl towards the phone but collapsed before she could reach it?

Karen was afraid someone might see her going through the gate. She could pretend to be delivering leaflets, but she had no leaflets. Perhaps if she went round the back of the garden, but as far as she could tell there was no back entrance, just a continuous wall. The house next door was much larger, and on the other side of the bungalow there was some kind of sub-station, owned by the electricity board, with warning signs like jagged orange lightning.

There was no-one about, not even a twitching curtain. The best thing would be to walk straight up to the front door, pretend to push something through the letter box, then go quickly round to the back, keeping as close as possible to the wall adjoining the next door house. Something Lydia Parfrey said had been preying on her mind. At the time she had thought very little about it, but recently it kept running through her head. *When I asked her to tell me more she just made some joke about a gooseberry bush.*

In the days before school libraries were stacked with books about 'where babies come from' people had told their children the stork brought them or they were found under gooseberry bushes. Esme had probably been making some kind of joke. Car thieves, gooseberry bushes; perhaps Lydia Parfrey had been right when she said Esme's mind had started to wander, but when Tessie and Mrs Livingstone talked about her they had never given that impression.

The garden at the back was mostly grass, but there was a patch for vegetables at the far end and an apple tree that looked as if it had been there for at least a hundred years. Karen approached a row of something that could have been onions, then tiptoed along a narrow path that led through to a compost heap and a small wooden shed. She had thought it would be easy to see if there were any gooseberry bushes, but since it was too early for fruit she had to try and remember what the leaves looked like. She recognised a small strawberry bed, then noticed some bushes that just possibly could be going to have gooseberries. The police would have searched the garden for clues. There was no sign of any footprints but it had rained several times during the last week and one night there had been the kind of downpour that would have washed away any marks.

She crouched between the wall and the bushes, carefully scraping away the topsoil with her hand, searching for something hard, a sharp edge, one of those metal money-boxes? If someone had known Esme had a large amount of money stashed away they would have assumed it was under the mattress, or a loose floorboard, or hidden in those cans that look like baked beans or vegetable soup but have lids that screw up tight. Had the intruder put pressure on her to tell him where it was and had she obstinately refused to say a word, even when he used physical force, even when she realised she was literally in danger of her life?

Next door a dog was barking, and a moment or two later Karen thought she could hear claws scratching on the adjoining fence. There was nothing under the bushes, or even nearby, not unless it was buried very deep. The shed door had a padlock but it hadn't been clicked shut. She went inside, brushing aside the cobwebs that clung to her face and hair, and found a trowel. Then she returned to the gooseberry bushes and continued digging for about ten minutes, anxious all the time in case someone noticed her, although she was almost certain she was hidden by the long grass that surrounded most of the vegetable bed. After replacing the earth and patting it down, she was just about to straighten up when she suddenly noticed something white and shiny. A piece of paper? It was more like the corner of a polythene bag or bin-liner. When she moved the earth nearby she must have disturbed it, although it was so small she would never have seen it if it hadn't been white.

Her heart was beating fast. Very slowly, carefully, she scraped back more earth, pulled the bag to the surface, then opened it and jumped back, stifling an involuntary scream. It was a dead animal. A cat Esme Fitch had buried, which had decomposed apart from its fur? A black one, that had gone brownish with age? She could smell it, she was sure she could. Then, as quickly as it had arisen, her panic subsided. Dead cats didn't have fur like that, not even long-haired Persians. Tipping up the bag she watched as the dark brown object slid to the ground. The hair was coarse but not very long, and the wig had a heavy fringe. She had seen it before, or another just like it, only last time it had been on somebody's head.

# *Eleven*

It was like standing on the edge of a swimming-pool, trying to pluck up the courage to jump into the cold, deep water. How many times during the day had she stood up, left the office, put her hand on the front door, then lost her nerve? The evidence she had collected might not be enough. A glimpse of someone in a black BMW, a wig found under a gooseberry bush. When she found the wig she had jumped to the obvious conclusion that it belonged to Lydia Parfrey. But obvious conclusions often turned out to be wrong and, in any case, how could she have been so sure there was a link between the wig and the violent attack on Esme Fitch? If Esme had been going around telling everyone Lydia was a fraud she had good reason to dislike her, but it still didn't explain why her wig – if her dark hair with its heavy fringe *was* a wig – had been buried in Esme's garden. Then there was the lie about Mary Davis, who could never have visited Lydia since she was housebound. Karen had thought about Selina's warning words, then pushed them out of her mind. Because Selina looked slightly strange and had a rather off-putting manner? Later, Karen had realised her mistake.

The phone started ringing. It was five-fifteen and her father was still on his way back from a business trip to London. She lifted the receiver and spoke the automatic words: 'Cady's Detective Agency. Can I help you?'

'Karen? Oh, I'm so sorry, but I didn't know what else to do.'

'Mrs Bowen?' Karen recognised the voice at once.

'It's Josh. The hospital rang half an hour ago. He's disappeared.'

'I don't understand. You mean he left the ward without anyone seeing him? Still, he was going home in the morning, anyway, wasn't he?'

'Yes, but he hasn't come back here.' She sounded as if she was crying. 'Can you think of anywhere, absolutely anywhere he might have gone. Mike's out searching, but I'll have to stay here, just in case. And there's something else – the worst thing . . . Before he left . . .' Her voice cracked.

'Yes?'

'Before he left he told one of the other patients, a boy of about the same age, that he was in trouble with the police, that he'd broken into a house but the owner had heard him and . . .'

'Don't worry,' said Karen, 'I'll go out and look for him straight away. I can't promise anything, but it is just possible I might know where he is.'

The police would be out in force. She had to get to Josh before they did. In spite of what Mrs Bowen had told her she was sure he was innocent. It was just a question of finding him, giving him a chance to explain.

It was raining hard, big drops that bounced off the lily leaves that covered that part of the canal. She thought about Lydia Parfrey's yellow candle. Then she thought about the dead cat that had turned out to be a thick, dark wig, and remembered Lydia's heavy make-up and false eyelashes. Perhaps she really did have a reason to disguise herself.

There was no-one about. The rain had driven people indoors and even the fishermen had packed up and left. At first she was afraid she wouldn't be able to find the backwater with the old barge, then she realised that she was on the wrong side of the canal and should have crossed the bridge near the incinerator.

The ground was spongy under her feet. She skirted the worst of the puddles, leaping from one side to the other, slipping on the wet grass but regaining her balance just in time. She had been so certain Josh would be on the barge. Now she wasn't sure. There could be dozens of places he visited and if he knew she had seen him on the barge that would probably mean he had decided to go and hide somewhere quite different. Why had he left the hospital? To avoid being collected by his parents in the morning?

But he couldn't just disappear. Sooner or later he would have to go home.

When the barge finally came into sight it looked deserted. There was not the slightest sign of any movement, but what had she expected? That Josh's face would be looking through one of the tiny windows? If he was there she would be the last person he wanted to see. If he was frightened enough he might turn nasty or, more likely, he would just push past her, run off and she would have no idea where he was going.

'Josh?' She stayed on the canal bank but leaned towards one of the broken windows. There was no reply. She called his name twice more, then stood for a moment, reluctant to go inside, although she knew she had to make sure. It was the first time she had studied the barge properly. It was painted grey but much of the paint had peeled off and she could see areas where the wood had started to rot. The sheet of greenish tarpaulin was lying on the ground, outside the cabin door. On the roof, if that was the right word for it, a rusty bike lay on its side, next to some broken flowerpots and a blackened chimney pipe.

Very cautiously she stepped on to the edge of the boat, then took a deep breath, jumped down, skirted round the tarpaulin and pulled open the door. He was sitting on the floor, with his knees pulled up in front of him and a blanket round his shoulders. He had heard her coming, and recognised her voice. He didn't look angry or afraid, just ill, defeated.

'Josh, what happened?' She crouched beside him. 'Your mother phoned. She's desperately worried.'

When he said nothing she moved to take hold of his shoulders, as if to shake him out of a trance, then remembered that one of his arms beneath the old, moth-eaten blanket was badly broken. 'Come on, you can tell me. That stuff you said to the boy in your ward – you haven't hurt anyone, I know you haven't.'

But how could she be so certain? Up to the time Mrs Bowen had told her about Stevie she had known so little about Josh. In her head she had turned him into a sad, lonely boy with no friends. Even seeing him in the garden of Mary Davis's house had never really convinced her he had anything to do with either of the violent crimes. Why? Because he didn't look the type? But people aren't always the way they look.

'Please tell me.' She knelt beside him. 'If you have done something bad it's still better to—'

'Stevie,' he muttered.

'Your brother? Yes, I know. Your mother told me about him. We met when she was on her way to visit him at the home.'

He stared at her, but he didn't ask how or where they had met.

'Please tell me,' she repeated. 'No, not about Stevie. About the time you were in Mary Davis's garden.'

He moved into a slightly more comfortable position. 'You saw me? When? I went there twice. Look, I didn't do anything. In the beginning I wanted them to think . . .'

'Yes.' She was trying to be patient but it was a struggle.

'Later, I suppose it got me thinking about who'd really done it, killed Miss Fitch, I mean.

Then after Mrs Davis was hurt . . .'

'But why did you run in front of Peter Quayle's car? You could've been killed. Was it because of your father? Because whatever you did he still went on pretending Stevie didn't exist.'

'Pretty stupid I suppose. I just want him to realise what he's doing to us all. The night before he'd said he didn't want Stevie's name mentioned, not when he was around.'

'But that's awful.'

Josh looked at her, as if to say: If you knew my father you wouldn't be that surprised, then he felt in his pocket and held something out in his hand. 'I found this at Mary Davis's. You'd think the police would have picked it up but it was under some leaves. I suppose they must have missed it. Anyway, it could've belonged to Mrs Davis except my mother said she was only interested in horses.'

'That's what your mother told you?'

'I suppose she got it from my father. She collected money for a horse sanctuary, and she had china horses and pictures of horses all over the house.'

Karen took the badge, turned it the right way up, then realised at once that she had seen it before. If the owner of the badge hadn't been uppermost in her mind she would probably have forgotten how it had been pinned to his sweatshirt. 'Wildlife Matters'. And a picture of an otter standing on its hind legs with its paws under its chin.

'Thought I'd find you here.' As the head came round the door Karen and Josh both scrambled to their feet.

Rain was dripping off Billy's short, reddish-brown hair. 'Two of you, eh? Who's your friend, Karen? I saw you running along the towpath, thought it was time we had a chat.'

'Josh knows nothing,' she said.

'Nothing about what, Karen?' Billy's voice was teasing, mocking. He sat down on a broad, low shelf that might once have acted as the base of a bed. 'I suppose you thought you were following in your father's footsteps,' he said. 'Trouble is, things don't always work out quite the way you want them to.'

She said nothing. She was thinking about the

way she had put off going to the police. Sitting in the office all day, incapable of making up her mind. Now it was too late.

'Seeing me in the car was a shame,' said Billy. 'I shouldn't have taken the risk, but that's me all over, can't resist it. Well, without taking risks life's a bit of a drag, wouldn't you say? Nice BMW 850, eh, but nicking them's far more fun than owning one. That way you get to drive the whole range.' He grinned at her. 'Anyway, after that what did you do? Started compiling a dossier to hand to the cops or your dad? Of course, even if Tessie hadn't hinted at what you were up to, I'd have had my suspicions. Hoping to follow in your father's footsteps, are you? I'd never have expected you to find car theft particularly interesting. Anyway, the police have a special unit, not that they ever get much beyond apprehending a few joy-riders. The big-time people like us are always a jump ahead.'

Josh was trying to stifle a cough. He looked very pale and his arm seemed to be hurting.

Billy laughed. 'Mentioning Mary Davis's visit to Lydia Parfrey, that was a bit of a mistake, but how was I to know the old bat was housebound?'

'You wanted me to think Lydia Parfrey had killed Esme Fitch and then broken into another of her client's houses? Why would she want to do—'

'Oh, nothing as complicated as that. It just amused me to see you running round in circles. There was no need for Mary Davis to end up in hospital. I hardly touched her, only did enough to make it look like the first break-in was a burglary gone wrong.'

Josh's coughing was getting worse. The blankets he had been sitting on when she found him looked mouldy and were almost certainly damp. In fact the whole barge smelled of rotting wood and mildew.

'So,' said Billy, 'this is your boyfriend, is it?' He held out his hand. 'Billy Henderson, and you're ... No, don't tell me, you're the kid Tessie was talking about, the boy with the weirdo brother.'

Josh sprang forward, but Billy grabbed him by the hair. 'Don't be an idiot. I haven't finished yet and she wants to hear the whole story, isn't that right, Karen? You know, Esme Fitch wasn't quite the sweet old thing you've been led to believe.'

'I never said she was.'

'Shh. Don't keep interrupting. She took rather a fancy to me, people often do, kept inviting me to her bungalow and giving me cups of tea and biccies. Trouble was, she couldn't leave it at that, thought she could get me back on the straight and narrow, reunited with my nice mummy and daddy, enrolled for another boring course. Then she took to following me about, only that turned out to be a big mistake.'

He stepped outside the cabin, looked all round, then returned, closing the door behind him.

'We had been given an order for a Ferrari. Handy really, when that Quayle bloke had one that just fitted the bill. Everything went like clockwork. The idiot used to park it in the same place on the same evening, and the special locking devices were a joke. Only trouble was Esme spotted me; just like you did, Karen, only she was quicker off the mark.'

'You were wearing a wig?'

'You got it. Threatened to make a helluva scene, she did. The thing came off when I was struggling to get free, and the silly cow wouldn't give it back.'

'You were in the car?'

'Just opening the driver's door. She made such a noise I drove off and left her to it. Only later she did something rather stupid. I called round at the bungalow, just to collect my property, and she wouldn't give it back, seemed to have decided to use it to blackmail me.'

Karen was breathing hard. 'I don't believe you,' she said. 'Anyway, what could you give her, you haven't any money.' But even as she spoke she realised that couldn't be true. He had plenty, the non-materialistic thing was just an act, a cover, something that made his double-life seem even more fun.

'Oh, she didn't want money, Karen, she just wanted me to live up to her fantasy. The charming young man who had made a few mistakes but could easily be put right. Of course, I never meant to kill her – she only had to tell me what she'd done with the wig.'

'But why did you want it so much? The police wouldn't have been able to prove anything.'

'Oh, they had their suspicions about me, and someone had given them a description of a man or a woman with thick dark hair with a fringe.'

'So why use that wig again?'

'Do me a favour. It was only after Esme had stolen it that the police began asking round for someone of that description. The wig you saw was rather different, wasn't it? Ash blonde, think it suited me? Not really, I haven't the right colouring. Might've looked better on your friend Peter Quayle.'

He had given up the jokey tone of voice and his eyes were cold and angry. Karen had no idea what he would do next, but when he started backing out of the cabin she was silly enough to allow herself to hope he was just going to walk away. He could leave the area, disappear for a time, then start up some other crazy scheme miles away in a completely different part of the country. How wrong could she be? The door closed with a bang and she heard something heavy rattle against it.

Josh jumped up and tried to pull it open with his good hand, then they turned to look at each other, both realising at the same time that Billy had fitted a heavy padlock. Karen rushed to check if the door was rotten, but the wood looked rock-solid so she left the cabin and started through the next one, then to the other end of the barge.

'It's no use,' called Josh. 'It's been sealed up. It'd be even harder to get out that end.'

They could hear noises. Josh put his ear to the cabin wall and as he listened she could see beads of sweat appear on his upper lip. 'He's making holes in it,' he said, 'below the waterline.'

'There must be another way out. The windows.'

Josh shook his head. 'They're too small, barely space for a dog to squeeze through.'

'You mean it's going to sink? No, it can't. Anyway the water's not that deep, if we keep calm, use our heads—'

'Deep enough,' he said. 'Some canals are quite shallow, but not this one.'

The hammering grew louder, then suddenly stopped. They strained their ears, listening for footsteps, trying to work out if Billy was walking away. There was silence, a total silence that was more frightening than the hammering had been. Then water started seeping through the floorboards and by the time they had both looked wildly around, searching for some kind of tool, anything they could use to try and force open the door, it had started to cover their feet.

# Twelve

'There's nothing we can do, there's no way out of here.' Josh was not the type to panic. He was simply stating a fact.

'There must be.' Karen had been kicking at the door, now she was opening drawers and cupboards, searching for something, anything, which would help them to escape. 'Anyway, the water will start going out through the windows.'

'Not when the boat sinks below the surface.'

The water had reached their ankles and was sloshing about on the floor. Karen had checked the three tiny cabins, but Josh had been right, there were no other exits and the windows were far too small. Of course, it was always possible someone might pass by within shouting distance. One of them should be leaning through a window all the time, but it was raining so hard there was very little chance anyone would be out for a walk.

'We could try pulling up the floorboards,' said Josh.

'What for? Look, you can't do anything with your arm in plaster. Just try and help me find something I can use as a tool. No, forget it, most of the drawers are empty, apart from a few oily rags. Think, there must be a way, we've got to *think*!'

Then she noticed the brass rail running the length of the cabin. It was at shoulder level and must once have been used for drying clothes, or perhaps just for decoration. She had a vague memory of a project they had done at her old primary school. A picture of the inside of a narrow boat; china plates on racks, a black stove with a white enamelled kettle. It was a long time since anyone had lived on this barge and there was no stove, although she could see from the scorch marks on the ceiling where it must once have stood.

She pointed at the rail and the two of them inspected the places where it fitted into the wall at either end. She could see Josh was going to ask what use it was, then he gave a sudden shout.

'This bit's loose. If we found something to chip at the wood we might be able to get it free, use it as a kind of battering-ram.'

The only things she had found were a rusty fork and a knife with its bone handle missing and just a pointed piece of metal left behind.

'Too blunt,' said Josh, 'it'll never work.'

'Well, it's all we've got.' She was shouting, made angry by fear. 'Look, I'll use the end where the handle's come off. It might work.'

The water was above their knees. It was cold and bits of debris from the floor of the cabin had floated to the surface.

Karen worked away at the hole where the rail had been fitted, gashing her finger when the knife slipped and feeling the blood drip backwards down her arm. Josh seemed to have given up but she refused to be beaten. He was attempting to pull open a drawer that had stuck when she tried it, but with only one hand, and wood that had expanded with the damp, he knew it was impossible. Most of the drawers and cupboards were now below water level. Some of the wood she was hacking at was rotten, but other parts had hardened with age. Taking hold of the brass rail she tried to rock it backwards and forwards, but it stayed stubbornly in place. Then, all of a sudden, she had an idea.

Balancing the knife on a high shelf, she sucked at the gash on her finger, then started swinging from the centre of the rod, with her legs pulled up from the ground. At first nothing happened – if only Josh had been able to help her – then she thought she felt a slight movement, but she might have just imagined it.

'Quick, Josh, have a look at that end over there. No, the other one.' And even as she spoke there was a loud crack as the place she had been working on crumbled and she fell back into the water.

It was easy enough to retrieve the brass rail, but it was so long it was virtually impossible to work up enough speed to make any impact. Over and over again she jammed it against the door, then dragged it back and did the same thing all over again. It wasn't going to work.

'The padlock's too strong,' she said, then, sounding far less terrified than she felt, 'but I'll have a go at one of the window frames, try to make a gap big enough to crawl through.'

Lifting the end of the rod she crashed it through the broken window, removing most of the remaining glass, then started banging it against the frame, first one side, then the other. At first nothing seemed to be happening, then all of a sudden the wood on the left-hand side started to splinter, along with a section of the wall. At the same moment water started coming through the window and she realised that in a matter of two or three minutes the barge was going to sink to the bottom and there would be nothing they could do.

Letting go of the rod she worked with her bare hands, pulling at the wood and feeling the rough edges scrape at her skin. A large lump came away and she lost her balance for a moment and fell against the wall.

'Now!' she yelled.

'There's not enough room.'

'Yes there is. Keep your bad arm as close to your body as you can. No, go on, go now!'

He hesitated for a moment, then did as she said. At the first attempt she was afraid he had become wedged. She couldn't see his face but knew he must be in pain. Wriggling himself free he tried again, but it was still no good, then forcing himself to make one last effort he shouted at her to push harder, and she watched as he managed to squeeze his shoulders through the gap, then fell on to the tow-path below, letting out a sound like a wounded animal.

She had water in her mouth. Easing her upper body through the broken window she felt her jeans catch on something and hold her fast. But terror was making her stronger than she could ever have imagined. Kicking out, and hurting her leg, she tried to push at the side of the barge with the palms of her hands, but there was very little of it above the surface any longer.

'Quick!' She could hear Josh's voice, but she

couldn't see him. Something sharp pierced her ankle. Water was rushing in her ears. Then all of a sudden she lurched forward, twisting sideways to try and break the fall, and landed with a thud on the path.

'Billy,' she yelled. 'Look for Billy.'

Josh stared at her in amazement. 'He's gone.'

'No, he could be nearby. He could be waiting for us.'

Josh shook his head. His face was streaked with dirt and he had a deep cut above one of his eyes. 'He'll be miles away by now,' he said, and it was the first time she remembered seeing him smile. 'He thinks we're dead.'

'I don't get it,' said Alex. 'Josh has a brother but his father never sees him?'

'He's going to soon,' said Karen. 'Stevie's coming home for the weekend. Josh says I can go and meet him.'

'Oh, I don't know,' said her mother, 'if there's been all this trouble with Josh's father I'm not sure they'll want you there, not until things are a little easier.'

'That's what Josh wants,' she said, 'and Mrs Bowen. Anyway, it's sometimes better if there's someone from outside the family, and I'd only be calling round for an hour or so.'

'You like this Josh then,' said Alex, giving her one of his stupid grins. 'From what you told us it sounded as if it was Peter Quayle who'd made the big impression.'

'Oh, him, he's all right, I suppose. Bit full of himself. There's some food in the fridge – lamb chops and new potatoes – but I'm afraid I have to go out.'

'Now? Already?' Her mother had her agonised expression. 'We've only been back an hour, and you haven't explained about the homeopath woman. How does she fit into everything?'

Karen smiled. 'She doesn't, she's just – well, she's OK, I suppose, if you like that kind of thing. Look, I won't be long, only I have to talk to Tessie.'

'Yes, but does it have to be right now?'

She nodded. 'She'd never admit it – I mean, she cares about chickens and calves and everything, well, we all do – but Billy was the main reason she was so involved with all the animal rights stuff. Think what she must be going through – now the police have caught up with him and he's safely under lock and key. Now she knows what he's *really* like.'

# A WATERY GRAVE
## A Karen Cady Mystery

*Penny Kline*

*The body of a young girl pulled from a reservoir. An unsolved crime. One suspect.*

Flame-haired Karen Cady, hoping to follow in her father's private detective footsteps, thinks she can solve the mystery. *Someone* must know who killed Natalie Stevens – and why.

An unexplained headline in a newspaper. A case that has remained unsolved for six months. A secret that someone is prepared to kill to keep . . .

# DEATHLY SILENCE
## A Karen Cady Mystery

*Penny Kline*

*Paul Challacombe: Clever, good at sport, popular at school. Missing.*

*Barbara Preston: Middle-aged. Not an enemy in the world. Murdered.*

Karen Cady is convinced there's a connection, but her father, a private detective, has long since given up the search. Pretending to write an article for the school magazine, Karen Cady starts to investigate.

Are Paul's family hiding something? Do they *really* want Paul found? And what was the secret Barbara told Paul shortly before her death? It's up to Karen to unearth a mystery some people would rather remained buried . . .

# A CHOICE OF EVILS
## A Karen Cady Mystery

*Penny Kline*

*Someone had got away with something really evil.*

Hannah Tremlett's father had a choice. To save his wife or his daughter from drowning. He saved Hannah. Now that her mother is dead, she is surrounded by a family silent in their grief, and unwilling to solve the mystery of her father's sudden disappearance. Only flame-haired Karen Cady can help.

Who wanted Hannah's mother dead? Why has her father now vanished? Is Hannah really to blame, or does the stranger in a purple sports car hold the key to a greater mystery? If he does, Karen had better not get too close . . .

# THE HOUSE OF BIRDS

*Jenny Jones*

Ominously overshadowing the village, Pelham Hall stands apart. Strange shrieks are heard from inside its walls.

Masked raiders thunder through the streets on huge black stallions. Their nightly catch is village children.

Harriet, orphaned and abandoned, sees her friends disappear, one by one.

Will she be next . . . ?